GHOST LAKE

Its real name is Caspar Lake, but people call it Ghost Lake. Years ago, a ferryboat went down in a storm, drowning everyone on board — and some say their souls have never rested . . . Beth Nolan travels to the nearby town at the invitation of an old school friend, but no sooner does she arrive than she is plunged into the murky depths of the brutal murder of a young woman. Beth must find answers — or risk joining the dead in the haunted depths of Ghost Lake . . .

V. J. BANIS

GHOST LAKE

Complete and Unabridged

LINFORD
Leicester

First published in Great Britain

First Linford Edition
published 2018

A catalogue record for this book is available
from the British Library.

ISBN 978–1–4448–3794–0

Published by
F. A. Thorpe (Publishing)
Anstey, Leicestershire

Set by Words & Graphics Ltd.
Anstey, Leicestershire
Printed and bound in Great Britain by
T. J. International Ltd., Padstow, Cornwall

This book is printed on acid-free paper

1

They called it Ghost Lake.

That is not its real name, of course. If you were to look on the maps, or checked in the tour books that you get from the auto club, you would find it listed as Caspar Lake. Along with the town that sits on its western shore, the town of Lake Caspar.

Which I had always thought a strangely ironic name for both town and lake. Caspar? That was the name of the ghost in the comic books, was it not? I remembered them from my childhood. But there was nothing comical about the tragic events at Ghost Lake.

That tragedy dated back to a time more than fifty years earlier, and the fateful crossing of a ferryboat. In those long-ago days, the only road around the lake was an old two-lane one with a single lane going in each direction. Depending upon the weather, and of course on how you drove, it could take as long as seven or eight hours to go around the lake on that narrow twisting road, with frequent stops along the way for intersections, railroad crossings, a few tiny villages with their pedestrian crossings, and the like. But the ferryboat made it across the water in little less than two hours. So of course, it was quite popular. It was, at that time, how practically everybody went from one side of the lake to the other. In less than two hours, too.

You did not even have to sit in your car for those not quite two hours if you did not choose to. At either end, you drove your car up a ramp from the dock into the belly of the beast. There you parked it in the slot designated for it. (For most crossings, reservations were recommended; otherwise, you took your chances on finding a space. Often there were none; it was that popular.) There, waiting crew members, usually moonlighting college students, chained it in place, after which you took an elevator to the upper level.

Up top, if you so wished, you could

simply stand by the rail on the open deck and watch the play of sun or moonlight upon the shimmering surface of the water. Some did. Or there were also three glass-enclosed cabins to choose from. One of them was a lounge where you could help yourself to free coffee from an always available urn. You could sit and sip, or read a magazine, also provided free, and usually the latest issue. Or you might engage in conversation with another passenger; many friendships were said to have started here, and not a few romances. Or if you were more of a loner, you could play solitaire with the decks of cards the company generously provided.

The second cabin was a mini-casino with gaming tables and slot machines, but the odds were so laughably poor — and this was so generally known — that few people frequented these. That cabin was, more often than not, mostly empty.

The third cabin, far and away the most popular of the three, held a bar, but it was generally referred to as 'the saloon.' Oh, there was food available, to be sure — mostly prepackaged sandwiches, canned soups, boxed doughnuts and the like. Nobody went there for the food, however. Instead, you could settle yourself comfortably on a barstool, or at one of the banquettes that lined the walls, and sip sidecars, which were popular in those days, or daiquiris, also popular, or Cuba Libres, which were nothing more than old-fashioned rum and Coke with a dash of lime juice. By the time you had finished a round, maybe two or so, you were at your destination on the other side of the lake.

A bell rang throughout the boat, half an hour before the vessel arrived at either of the piers, alerting everyone that it was time to retire to their vehicles and prepare to drive them down the exit ramp and out of the boat once the ferry had docked.

Sometimes it happened that a driver had enjoyed himself too much in the bar, and was in no condition to drive. If they was traveling from east to west, they were most likely only going the short distance, a handful of blocks only, to the town's then only notable hotel, the Lodge at the Lake, where everyone who was anyone

4

stayed. There were no accommodations on the eastern shore. It was generally supposed that anyone going in that direction already had a home nearby and, more often than not, was being met at the pier by a wife or family member, and so the drinks in the saloon were of no great consequence.

The company that ran the ferry line had even prepared for that eventuality, however, if discreetly. A few bills, folded neatly, slipped into the hand of a crew member (and they were always close at hand at these times, just in case) would buy one a chauffeur, if only for that brief trip. In which case, another crew member followed in a company car to bring the chauffeur back to the pier after his duty was done.

With so much careful attention to the needs and wants of their passengers, the ferryboat line was doing a booming business. A fleet of no fewer than six boats crossed continuously back and forth across the lake daily, day and night, their deck crews shouting and waving to one another as they passed, and sometimes making dates for later. The trip from east to west was the more popular one. It was then that the most coffee got drunk in the lounge, and the bartender in the saloon was kept his busiest.

All was well, then, until that fateful night.

It was nearing midnight. The boat was traveling east to west, but this was the last crossing of the day, and with that and the inclement weather, the boat was filled to far less than its capacity. Which was the only good thing anyone could find to say about the trip afterward.

It was also storming, hard. No one stood by the railings outside, and only a pair of solitary travelers sat in the glass-enclosed lounge, one of them drinking coffee and reading a magazine and the other, yes, playing solitaire. But for a few bored attendants, no one was in the gaming room.

Lightning flashed often and thunder boomed. Violent winds lashed the lake's waves into great troughs and white crested peaks. The rain, great torrents of it, beat a staccato tattoo upon the deck and knocked insolently at the windows of the cabins, as if demanding entrance.

In the saloon, where most had quickly retired upon boarding, only the bravest of the passengers stood or sat at the bar proper, clinging to its padded leatherette surface to keep themselves upright. Most of patrons had taken instead to the banquettes, where they clutched at the edges of their upholstered seats and giggled nervously to see their glasses slide about on the surface of the table as the boat heaved and wallowed from one side to the other, at the surge of the roiling waters.

Afterward, it was deemed fortunate that there had been so few passengers aboard. Relatively speaking, of course. On a good crossing, in daylight, and without the storm, there might have been two hundred passengers in the bar alone, and easily that many more elsewhere about the boat. As it was, counting all, there only a bit more than a hundred hardy souls crossing the lake on that occasion.

In the hold below, the cars rocked

frantically back and forth in imitation of the drinks above, as if, like wild animals, they wanted to be loosed from the chains holding them in place; until finally, one of them did indeed escape. It broke free of its chains and, on the next tilt, went right through a wall, leaving a hole in the hull the size, it was said, of a car. Through which in turn the water poured copiously into the boat. Poured so copiously, in fact, that the crippled boat sank within minutes. Within twenty minutes, according to later reports. Too quickly for any rescuers to reach those hapless passengers, though at least two of the line's other boats tried valiantly to respond to the distress call, racing at full speed across the water.

They were too late, as it happened, to save those poor souls who only minutes before had been laughing among themselves and trying to catch errant glasses as they slid this way and that at the whims of the waves. And now suddenly they were plunged into that icy water, rain beating down upon their heads, trying desperately to find something, anything, to hold on to, to save themselves. In vain.

Counting crew and all, nearly one hundred and fifty people drowned that night. The ferryboat line never recovered, and within two years it was out of business. No one wanted any longer to sail across the lake. What did it matter how long it took to make the drive? You were in no danger of drowning, at least. And when the new road was completed to great fanfare, and that was no more than ten years later, you could circle the lake in fewer than five hours. The new highway saw much traffic, starting with its first day.

In time, someone started another ferryboat line. This one was much more utilitarian, with no gambling rooms and no bars, though there was a row of vending machines on the upper deck that dispensed coffee or tea or hot chocolate. Of course, it was much safer too. The cars in the hold were nestled between great slabs of batting that kept them firmly in their place, and the hulls were triple-reinforced, just in case another vehicle went astray.

A single boat, large and ungainly, trudged across the lake twice each day, never at night, and not when the weather was bad, at which times crossings were delayed or even canceled. Some, the practical ones, once again chose that means of crossing because it still saved a couple of hours over making the trip around by car; but the old glamor of crossing the lake in style was gone, never to return.

Caspar Lake, the watery expanse and the town of Lake Caspar (which reversal of names no one had ever quite explained), both survived the loss of their tourist appeal, if barely. The years that followed the tragedy were lean ones for both. Many businesses closed, and those that remained pared back their offerings to match the new reality.

This was until the rumors began to circulate about the ghosts. It was said that late on some nights, when it was stormy and the winds blowing, you could hear them: the ghosts of those lost passengers, crying for help, begging to be saved. Some intrepid souls, crossing the lake at night in their own speedboats, which by then had become more common, swore they saw some of the dead passengers rising from the depths of the lake and signaling frantically to be rescued. No one, it was said, stopped or even slowed for them. Who would?

And though the name of the town and of the lake remained, officially at least, unchanged, many of the locals began to refer to it as Ghost Lake. And the tourists, intrigued by the stories of ghosts, began to come back. As people will do, at the chance of a good scare. Which no doubt explains the ongoing popularity of the roller coaster, and other rides designed to frighten.

And I? In time, I found myself in grave danger of becoming one of the dead . . . those ghosts rising from the depths of the water to frighten passersby.

2

I came to the lake at the invitation of my old friend, Sarah Gladstone. Sarah and I had been at school together, one of those to which families in those days sent their daughters, ostensibly for a better education, but more realistically, one supposes, to have them out of one's hair. We had been school chums, special friends, in the defensive way that the less popular students sometimes bonded together.

She was Jewish, only a small fraction Jewish actually (a mere twig somewhere well back on the family tree), but still the only student in that wasp citadel with a Jewish name; and I was there on a scholarship, a poor girl in a school populated by the daughters of moneyed society. Both of us were fatherless. Sarah's had walked out on wife and children, and died not long after in an auto accident. Quite un-mourned, Sarah liked to assure me.

I had never really known either of my parents, who had died when I was a mere baby. I was taken in by a spinster aunt, Aunt Thelma. My father's sister. Aunt Thelma had seen to it that I had everything that I needed in physical terms, but she was incapable of even the slightest show of affection. That was not her fault. Hers was not a warm or nurturing nature.

And no sooner had Aunt Thelma learned of Miss Parker's School for Young Ladies, and learned that I qualified for a scholarship there, than off I went. I should probably say that I minded hardly at all. I was like a an unresisting leaf, carried along the edges of a stream without ever sailing into its main currents, caught briefly in this little harbor, until moved grudgingly along to the next. Miss Parker's was just another haven for me. I would probably have survived just as well without Sarah's friendship, but I was grateful for it all the same.

We were the only friend either of us had there, and because she was a year ahead of me in school, my last year without her was lonelier than I might have expected. She must have known this, because she wrote to invite me to come visit her at Caspar Lake (no Ghost Lake for Sarah) for summer vacation when my final year ended. She shared a two-bedroom cottage there with her widowed mother and her sister Anabelle. Anabelle, who was for the most part her mother's caretaker, shared her mother's room; the other, much smaller bedroom, was Sarah's. There was a younger brother who, it seemed, slept on a sofa in the living room.

Since space in their cottage was at a premium, Sarah warned me that if I wanted to stay with them, I was more than welcome, but the best she could offer me was a cot on the enclosed back porch, which was screened and perfectly habitable, but had to be shared with their laundry facilities. On the other hand, though its circumstances were much changed these days, the Lodge, as it was now known, was still in business, if I preferred.

This was not, in fact, my first visit to the lake. I had come before, also at Sarah's invitation, and not long after we had first become friends, so I suppose I was eight, perhaps, or nine, and Sarah a year older. I had only vague memories, but I did remember the Lodge, a huge faux-log building with a wrap-around veranda furnished with rockers and chairs. Just what one might envision as a welcoming country inn, both rustic and comfortable.

I wrote back to say I would get a room for myself at the Lodge. I understood that it was not as grand as it had been in the past (when I almost certainly would not have been able to afford it), and that there was even a modern motel now at the one end of town. But the Lodge was more to my taste, and cheaper than that motel besides. And with the job I had taken, secretary at a legal firm, I had saved enough, if I was careful of the pennies, to give myself a month's splurge.

I flew into the city of San Bernardino, which offered the nearest airport to the town of Lake Caspar. Sarah met me at my arrival for the drive up the mountain.

'Do you remember when you were here before?' she asked me once we were on the road.

'Very little. We were terribly young, as I recall.'

'I was ten. So I think you must have been nine.'

'That's about what I thought, too.'

'And I suppose you've heard about our ghosts? They're new since you were here before.'

'Yes, I've heard about them,' I admitted. 'Not a lot but a bit, though. Spirits, so I have heard, that rise up from the water and shout 'Boo' at passing boats. I may as well tell you, I'm going to be very disappointed if I don't get to see them while I'm here.'

'Beth, love, don't be facetious,' she scolded me. 'You'll find that lots of people take the ghosts very seriously.'

'Then I see no problem with arranging a meeting for me,' I said. I was one of those who would ride a roller coaster anywhere, any time. Or see a ghost, if one was on offer.

'Hmm. Well, for starters, you would have to be out on the lake,' she said. 'These are strictly water spirits.'

'But you have a boat, don't you?'

'We do. It's an old outboard. It's not very chic, I'm afraid. But what I really meant was, you'd have to be out on the lake at night.'

'So? I'm not afraid of the dark. Are you?'

'No, but I fear it's a bit more complicated than that. I meant, not just at night, but you'd have to be out in a storm as well. It seems that's the only time people see them, in the dark and in a storm. They're apparently not very accommodating, our ghosts.'

'Oh. And I suppose what you're trying to say is that you're not going to take me out at night, in a storm, to see these ghosts?'

'A storm? In our old tub? I don't think you'd much like that idea, once you've seen our boat.'

'So you're saying there won't be any cheap scares for me?'

'Well, you're going to meet my sister,

Anabelle,' she said with a laugh. 'I don't think she was here the last time you visited. She had a job down the hill then, as I recall. But she's here now, and there are people who find her plenty scary. I'll even ask her if she can put on a sheet for your benefit, if you like.'

'Oh. I forgot about Anabelle.' What I really had forgotten was that the two shared not a trace of sisterly affection. 'And wait, isn't there a brother too?'

'Mike? Yes, the kid brother. Which label he hates, of course, now that he's nineteen. At that age, you don't want to be known as the kid anything.'

We both laughed at that. 'So true,' I said, and then asked, 'Is he living at the cottage too? I think you said something about his sleeping on the living room sofa.'

She was so long answering, I thought at first she had not heard me, and I was about to repeat the question when finally she said, 'No. He was at the house and sleeping on the couch, but now he's got a place of his own. A little trailer.'

'Good for him. Boys like having their

own space. The last thing they want is a big sister breathing down their necks.'

'I think that's how he feels about things. Or did.' She paused again, and then added, but speaking slowly, 'There was a girl there with him for a while. Laurie. Laura Rainey. Sort of his girlfriend, I guess. Or maybe sort of not.'

'But she's not there now,' I said, and sighed. 'It happens. I had a boyfriend of my own a year ago, just after school let out, but he's gone now too. Is Mike devastated over the breakup?'

'It wasn't exactly what you might call a breakup.' She said this very cautiously, as if she were testing each word as she said it.

'Oh?' I looked a question at her, but she was busy driving, her eyes carefully glued to the road ahead.

'She's dead,' she said, taking her eyes off the road just long enough to give me a quick glance, which told me that there was something particularly significant in this news.

'And?'

'And?' she echoed me.

'And there's more to this than you've told me. From the way you said that, I'd guess a lot more.'

She sighed, her eyes back on the road, for which fact I really was grateful. We were in the mountains, as I have said, and just then negotiating a wicked curve, with a terrible fall awaiting us just outside my window. The cliff's edge was only inches beyond the glass, or so it seemed to me, looking out.

'She was killed,' she said, and then, added quickly, 'They think Mike killed her.'

'Mike?' I cried.

'They're certain he murdered her, in fact,' she amended. 'At least that's what the sheriff thinks.'

'I don't believe that. I know it's been forever, and I only met him that one time, when they came up to school to see you. He couldn't have been more than fourteen, or maybe fifteen at the time. But he was such a quiet young man. I simply can't imagine him murdering anyone.'

'You met him twice, as a matter of fact.

In a manner of speaking.'

'Oh wait, you're right, of course. But he was only a baby when I was here before, so that doesn't really count, does it? And the second time, well, I would've said he was as harmless as a mouse. And about as timid, too.'

'The sheriff seems to think he's more of a rat.'

'Now you have to tell me the story. What happened?'

'That kind of depends,' she said, 'on whose story you believe. They were down by the lake that night, at the little park there, the one with the sort-of beach. It was winter, so there was no one else there at the time. And they were quarreling, it seems. On those points, at least, everyone agrees.'

'But not what follows?'

'Right. Mike says she fell. He says that she must have hit her head on a rock when she landed. He says she was alive when he left her, and he walked back alone to his trailer.'

'And the sheriff says otherwise.'

'Of course. They say her head was

bashed in. Not like she had hit it on a rock, although the ground right about there is plenty rocky. More like, they say, someone had beaten her to death. The sheriff says it was Mike, maybe with a rock.'

'But what motive could he have?'

'I have no clue. He doesn't talk about it. He won't much, except to say he didn't kill her.'

'And of course they don't believe him. The poor kid.' I sighed. 'It's bad enough losing someone you love, without all the rest of it.'

'He says they weren't, you know.' She threw me another of those quick sideways glances. This time, at least we were on one of the few straight stretches of the road.

'No, I don't know. Weren't what?'

'He says they weren't lovers, I mean. They were just friends. He keeps insisting that she was a good Catholic girl.'

'But they did live together? That part of it is true, surely.'

'Yes. For about two months. Before it happened. But if you want my opinion, I think he did love her, regardless of what he says. They'd known one another since they were kids. She used to live next door to us, ages ago. Not where we are now. At our old place. I think he'd been in love with her for years.'

'But you think she didn't love him in return?'

'I . . . ' She hesitated. 'I don't know. It's hard to say. And things were a bit more complicated than that.'

'In what way, complicated?'

'I think . . . well, to be honest, I think maybe I have said more than I should have. I don't really know anything, anyway, so whatever I said, I'd only be repeating gossip. And you know how I feel about that.'

We had too often been a source of gossip ourselves when we were in school together. There were those, and not a few of them, who suggested that Sarah and I had been more than just friends at the time. I had mostly laughed at the idea, but Sarah had been, and often, genuinely angry.

It had begun to rain, a few droplets

only at the start, but quickly coming down harder. Sarah reached to turn on the wipers.

'Maybe you'll get to see to see those ghosts after all,' she said. 'Or hear them, at least, unless you plan on going for a long swim in the rain.'

We rode for a long time in silence, broken only by the regular clickity-clack of the wipers on the windscreen.

That much I did remember about Lake Caspar: it rained, a lot.

3

Something I had forgotten, though, was the lack of sidewalks and curbs. The town's main drag had them, presumably for the convenience of tourists. But as soon as you turned off that, onto one of the side streets, they disappeared.

It was all about the money, one supposes, or the lack of it. Sidewalks were expensive to build, I imagined; and after the boating tragedy and the loss of tourists business, the town had had little enough cash to go around. Streets were a necessity, so they were tended to; sidewalks, however, were a luxury the town of Lake Caspar could not now afford.

We stopped first at the cottage. I looked at it from the shelter of the car. 'This isn't the house I remember,' I said.

'No, it isn't. I told you. We moved since you were here. Not terribly long after that, I think. Anyway, we're stopping here first, before I take you to the Lodge, because Mom wants to see you,' she said. 'She insisted on it.'

'And Anabelle?'

'She probably doesn't. She isn't the most sociable person. But if you're here for any length of time, you're going to run into her sooner or later, so you might as well get the initial shock over with.'

The rain, which had been coming down hard during our drive, had lessened a bit, but it was growing dark as evening settled in. 'There's a poncho on the back seat there,' she said. 'I brought it for you just in case. You might want to slip that on.'

I found the poncho where she pointed, and scrabbling around in my seat, got it and slipped it over my head. 'But what about you?' I asked. 'Aren't you going to get wet?'

'From this?' She waved a hand at the windshield and the rain, now no more than a drizzle, and laughed. 'When you live here at the lake, you get used to water, water, everywhere.'

'And all the boards did shrink,' I

added. At school, we'd had to memorize 'The Rime of the Ancient Mariner', which both of us had hated.

She laughed. 'You haven't forgotten, I see.'

'I'll be quoting that poem for the rest of my life, I think.'

'Me too,' she said with another laugh. 'Come on, follow me.'

With that, she threw her door open and ran for the cottage's front door. I pulled the hood of the poncho over my hair and ran after her.

We were laughing like a pair of silly kids as we burst through. 'You can hang the poncho there,' she said, still giggling and pointing at some wooden pegs on the wall just inside. 'The floor here is linoleum, so the drips won't hurt anything.'

'What on earth is all that racket?' a voice said from within, and a moment later Anabelle came in from the kitchen, nothing more than an ell off the front room. She saw her sister and said in a not altogether welcoming tone, 'Oh, it's you.'

'And Beth,' Sarah said. 'This is Beth

Nolan, from Miss Parker's School for Young Ladies.'

At least Anabelle managed a smile for me, if not a cheery one. 'How are you, Beth Nolan from Miss Parker's School for Young Ladies? Welcome to Lake Caspar. I'm Anabelle.'

'Thanks, I'm fine. And you?'

'Oh, feeling a little bit shopworn, but I'm mostly okay.'

I had forgotten: Sarah had talked often about how intimidating Anabelle could be. She was a big woman, surely almost six feet tall, with wide shoulders and sturdily built over a generous frame. She was wearing a frilly dress, presumably hoping it would make her look more feminine, but the result was just the opposite. With her hair cut short and her stocky build, she looked like nothing so much as a poorly costumed drag queen.

At that moment a white toy poodle dashed out of a nearby room, dancing and yipping as she came.

'You,' Anabelle said as if it were a curse. She reached down, scooping the little dog up in one hand and opening the back door with the other. She tossed the dog outside and slammed the door behind her.

'Will she be all right?' Sarah asked.

Anabelle made a face. 'With any luck, the coyotes will get her.'

'Anabelle, you can't mean that,' Sarah cried.

'Shopworn?' I repeated, trying to head of the impending argument.

'Oh, pay me no mind. I'm just tired, is all,' Anabelle said. 'And don't fret,' she told Sarah. 'The dog will be fine. The coyotes don't come up this close to the house. They shy away from people. From me, anyway.'

'It's no wonder you're tired, either,' Sarah said in a solicitous voice, the dog seemingly forgotten. 'You try to do too much, Anabelle. I'll bet money you were in there just now scrubbing the kitchen floor or something equally backbreaking. Why don't you just relax for a spell? You know, you could go and sit in the living room and watch some television for a while, for Pete's sake.'

'Television?' Anabelle scoffed. 'I'm sure

there's nothing on the idiot box that I'd want to watch.'

'Soap operas, maybe,' Sarah suggested without much enthusiasm.

'I hate soap operas,' Anabelle said. 'Besides, someone has to look after things.' To me, she said, 'Mother's health isn't very good. She needs a lot of attention. That means me.'

From further inside the house, a voice called, 'Is that you, Sarah?' A moment later, Mrs. Gladstone — Greta, though I had always called her Mrs. Gladstone — appeared. 'I thought I heard your voice. Oh, Beth, hello. Sarah told me you'd be here. I'm so glad you decided to come for a visit.'

Frankly, though I knew full well Greta Gladstone had always been a chronic complainer, I did not think she looked very good. She had lost weight since the last time I had seen her, although admittedly that had been some years earlier. But it was not just the weight, or the toll of the passing years. She looked wan and drawn, and her complexion had a gray cast to it.

But I kept those thoughts to myself. 'Mrs. Gladstone, hello. It's good to see you too,' I said instead. 'How are you?'

She sighed and gave me a forlorn look. 'Oh, about as well as can be expected, I suppose. My heart, you know.' She put a hand up to pat at her ample bosom. The ring on her finger glinted wickedly.

I had forgotten *the ring*, as Sarah and I used to laughingly refer to it, with verbal italics, a diamond certainly big enough to satisfy anyone's definition of 'vulgar,' surrounded by emerald chips. Mrs. Gladstone had always taken inordinate pleasure in showing it off, and I suspected at this moment that her gesture, patting at her bosom, was not entirely chance.

'Did Daisy come this way?' she asked of the room in general, and said to me, 'Daisy's my poodle.'

'A little white one?' I asked. 'Yes, she . . . ' I paused, not sure if I should mention Anabelle's treatment of the dog.

'Daisy's outside,' Anabelle said, saving me the trouble. 'Doing her business.'

There was a scratching at the back door just then, and a pitiful whine.

31

'It sounds like she's ready to come in now,' Mrs. Gladstone said. 'Sarah, let her in, please.'

'Of course,' Sarah said, smiling sweetly at her sister and going to open the kitchen door. Daisy dashed in, shot Anabelle an angry look and, seeing Mrs. Gladstone, ran right to her.

'Oh, there you are, my Snooky-ukums,' Mrs. Gladstone cried, lifting the dog off the floor. She did the bosom-patting number again. 'Oh, you'll give me a heart attack yet, you little devil.'

'Now, Mother,' Sarah said, 'you know perfectly well Doctor Webster says as long as you take your medicines as prescribed, you'll live to be a hundred.'

'Oh, that old quack,' she said with a dismissive gesture, waving *the ring* in case I had not fully appreciated it before. 'He's just thinking about his money. He hopes I do live that long so I can keep paying his outrageous fees, is all.'

'Well, it does give him a motive for keeping you alive,' I said brightly. 'And I can see you've lost some weight since the last time I saw you. Did you mean to?'

'I don't suppose at my age anybody ever minds dropping a few pounds,' she said. 'But I think the credit goes mostly to the medications I take.'

'What are you on?' I asked. 'Maybe I'll try them.'

'She takes a raft of pills,' Anabelle was quick to answer for her mother, 'but the most important one, the one I really have to keep track of, is Lanoxin. Or Digoxin, by its real name.'

I had to think for a moment; I had once dated a medical student, so I knew most medications by their proprietary name. 'Digitalis,' I said.

'Very good. That's right,' Anabelle said, nodding. 'Our old friend, Mister Foxglove.'

'You're entirely correct, too,' I said. 'You do need to keep careful track of that. It has to be carefully monitored.' I turned to Mrs. Gladstone. 'But if you're not happy with your doctor, why are you still seeing him? Surely there are other doctors available. Didn't I read that there's a hospital here in Lake Caspar?'

'Not a real hospital. It's only a clinic.

One of those chain things,' she corrected me. 'And they aren't the best in the world either, if you ask me. If it wasn't for Anabelle looking after me, I don't know what I'd do.'

'She's very lucky then,' I said, speaking to Anabelle, 'to have you taking such good care of her.'

'It's not all that much work, really,' Anabelle said, her tone and her facial expression making it perfectly clear that she thought otherwise. 'Mostly it's just making sure she takes her medications at the right time, in the right order. Especially, as you say, that Lanoxin.'

'Which I confess I'm no good for,' Sarah said. 'I try, but I can never keep track of things. Mother would forget and then I'd forget too, and wouldn't we be in a pretty pickle?'

'You forget things because you don't care enough to remember them,' her mother said. 'That's all it is.'

'I care,' Sarah said. 'But my memory is a sieve.'

Her mother only grunted at this. 'You've heard about Mike, I suppose?' she asked, turning to me.

'Some of it. And I'm sure everything will work out. If, as he says, he's innocent . . . '

'If?' She gave me a scandalized look. 'Of course he's innocent, isn't he Sarah? Anabelle? You both agree with me, don't you? You know he didn't kill that girl.'

They were both quick to insist that their brother was indeed innocent.

'See.' Mrs. Gladstone gave me a triumphant look.

Not wanting to be dragged into a lengthy discussion on that subject, I said quickly, 'I do see. And I hate to run, but I probably should head over to the Lodge before it gets any later and see about getting myself checked in. I wouldn't want them to give my room to someone else.'

Mrs. Gladstone snorted dismissively. 'I don't think you need to worry too much about that. I doubt they're ever booked to capacity these days.'

'It'd seem the ghosts have scared a lot of people off,' Anabelle said.

'And attracted others,' Sarah added.

'People do love mysterious happenings, it seems. Happily the tourists have started coming back lately. I suppose all of them hope they'll get to see the ghosts.'

'Well, I for one hope I get to see one or two of them while I'm here,' I said. 'I'll be very disappointed if I don't.'

'Don't bank on it. And you're probably right,' Sarah said, 'You should get on over to the Lodge. I think the registration desk closes down early. Come on, I'll drive you there.'

'That's kind of you, but if memory serves, it's not all that far. I can walk.'

'If you do, take my friend with you,' Anabelle said. She indicated a baseball bat leaning against the wall by the door. 'I never go for a walk without him.'

'Why on earth would I need that?' I asked.

'You don't listen to the news?' Anabelle asked, aghast. 'Or read the papers? Women get assaulted all the time. It happens every day.'

'I do follow the news. But surely here in this town there's no problem.' I spread my hands.

'You're thinking that because we're only a small town, there's probably no crazies here? Hah! The creeps are everywhere these days, believe me. I see them hanging around everywhere I go, when I was down the hill, and right here in Lake Caspar, too. Don't kid yourself: men are just looking to catch an unwary woman out on her own.'

'Even here?'

'Even here.' Anabelle nodded grimly. 'But believe me, if one of them tries anything on me, he'll be eating his teeth. That's why I carry my friend there with me.'

'I'm not sure I'd want to use a baseball bat to defend myself,' I said. 'I can't imagine having some man eating his teeth, as you put it.'

'That's not all, either. I have a shotgun, too, in the closet there.'

'A shotgun?'

'Not to carry with me, of course. That's just in case anybody starts getting ideas about a houseful of women all alone here with no man to protect them. And believe me, I know how to use it, too.'

'Come on, it's getting late,' Sarah said again emphatically. I got the impression this conversation was not a new one.

I turned obediently to go and stopped by a large planter of pink flowers that stood just by the door. 'Oh, aren't these pretty? And don't they smell sweet, too?' I bent down to take a sniff of the showy blossoms.

'Those are oleanders,' Anabelle said with a proud smile. 'Some people can't grow them where the winters are cold, but I've had these for years now. And look how well they're doing.'

'You have a green thumb,' her mother said.

Anabelle shrugged. 'I baby them, is all it is. Later in the summer, I'll carry this planter outside where they can soak up lots of sunshine; but as soon as the weather starts to turn cool, back inside they come. Most people wait for the first frost, but by then the damage is already done, in my opinion. They're very climate sensitive, it seems to me.'

'Oleanders?' I took a step back from the flowers. 'But aren't they dangerous?'

'To horses, if they eat them,' Anabelle said. 'Don't worry, you won't get sick from just smelling them. And no, we don't have any horses to worry about.'

'They're toxic for people too, if they ingest them,' Sarah said. 'Maybe not fatal, but people can get sick.'

'That's true. But I hope everyone here has better sense,' Anabelle said. 'Mother, are you going to start eating the oleander plants when I'm not looking?' She gave a coarse laugh to show that she was joking.

Mrs. Gladstone laughed too. 'Heavens, no. Though they smell lovely, don't they? I have to say I've been tempted sometimes. Not to eat them, but I've wondered if you could make tea with them.' She looked hard at the pink flowers.

'I wouldn't try,' Sarah said. 'I doubt it's safe.'

'Mother drinks herbal tea,' Anabelle said to me. 'If you were wondering.'

'But not oleander tea,' her mother said. 'I drink different flavors for different effects. The chamomile, for instance, is very soothing. It helps me to sleep, so I have that in the evening. And there's a morning one too, I forget what's in it, but it perks me up.'

'Come on, Beth,' Sarah said, 'Let's us head for the Lodge. They're not likely to give away your room; Mother's right about that. But I think you have to sign up if you expect dinner.'

'I *am* getting hungry,' I said.

'And I'd invite you back here to eat with us, but most of the time we just open cans or pop something into the microwave. You'll like Mrs. Gershon's cooking a lot better than mine, anyway, trust me. She's the proprietress. And a fine cook.'

'Speak for yourself. I can cook,' Anabelle said. 'And it's not all cans and microwaves either. But Sarah's right, that is what's in store for us tonight: ready meals. Later, when I've had time to get to a market, we'll have you back for a proper meal, Beth. If you'd like?'

'I'd love to.' I took the poncho, now almost dry, off the peg where I had hung it earlier. 'It was good seeing everyone.'

'I hope we see more of you,' Mrs. Gladstone said.

'You will. I promise. I plan on being here for a month or so,' I said, heading out the door, which Sarah had opened for me.

4

When we were back in the car, Sarah said, 'I'll bet you're glad now you booked at the Lodge. Those two could drive a preacher to drink, couldn't they?'

'They're okay,' I said. 'But I can see how they could wear on you, as an everyday thing.'

'You said it.'

'Sarah,' I said when we were on our way, 'if you don't mind terribly, I'd kind of like to say hi to Mike, too, before we go to the Lodge.'

'I was hoping you might,' she said. 'Plus I know he'd be tickled to see you. And his trailer is just a couple of blocks away, so it's not like it's out of the way. Well, I suppose you could say that about almost anything here in Lake Caspar. The town isn't that big, if you'll remember.'

She turned right at the corner, and at the next street right again, and after no more than a block she pulled up in front of a small trailer on a well-kept lot. Here again there were no sidewalks and no curbs.

'This is Mike's place,' she said. 'Do you want me to wait out here while you go in to say hi? Or I can come back later to get you, if you want to stay a bit longer.'

'Like you said, this town isn't very big,' I said. 'That's the main drag there, isn't it? At the traffic light? And if I remember correctly, if I turn left there, the Lodge is no more than three or four blocks down?'

'Only two,' she said. 'But they are rather longish blocks.'

'Not that long, surely,' I said. 'I think I can manage that. I do have the poncho you loaned me. And my cell phone. With your number in it, just in case the walk proves too much for me, which I doubt.'

'Okay, if you're sure. But don't hesitate to call me if you change your mind. As you've seen, the house is no more than a couple of blocks away. And if by chance I don't see you tonight, I'll give you a jingle in the morning.'

'But not too early, okay? I *am* on vacation.'

'Not too early, of course. And we'll do something together. Maybe go for a ride on the lake.'

'But no ghosts?'

'Not in the daytime. I told you, our spirits like to play hard to get. They only come out when it suits them.'

I was out of the car before I remembered. 'Oh, my suitcase,' I said. 'It's still in the trunk of your car. Should I get that?'

'Don't worry about it. I'll drop it off at the Lodge for you on my way home. They'll keep a watchful eye on it.'

'And maybe while you're there, tell them I'll be a bit late for dinner?'

'Will do. I'll tell Mrs. Gershon, okay?'

'Thanks.'

She gave me a final wave and drove away. I waited until her taillights had disappeared around the next corner. Then I turned and made my way up a stone-lined walk to the door of the trailer.

Mike answered at once, surprised to see me at his door. 'Oh, it's Beth Nolan, isn't it?' he said. 'I heard you were coming into town.'

'Yes. And if Mohammed won't come to the mountain,' I said, 'then the mountain must come to Mohammed. Are you busy?'

'Not very likely,' he said with a grin. 'I just made a fresh pot of coffee. Would the mountain care for a cup?'

'Sounds good to me.'

'Well, come on in, then.' He threw the door wide and made an expansive gesture.

Inside, he waved his hand at a dinette built into the front end of the trailer. 'Have a seat. I would've been there, you know, at Mom's, to welcome you to Lake Caspar, but I'm kind of on restriction just now. I'm not supposed to leave the trailer without permission.'

'Aren't you supposed to be wearing leg chains, then?' I asked. 'And dragging a big metal ball around behind you? Like they do in the movies, I think. Or the cartoons, anyway.'

'In Lake Caspar? Nothing that high-tech here, I'm afraid,' he said with a laugh. More seriously, he said, 'And I'm allowed to go out, but I have to have

45

Mother or Sarah with me as a chaperone, and that's only to go around town. But if I want to go anywhere alone, or any distance, then I have to call the sheriff and get permission. It's kind of like being in detention back in school.'

'Oh, I remember that. At Miss Parker's we had to sit in study hall. And actually study, too.'

He gave me a somewhat sheepish look. 'I guess you heard about my . . . well, about what happened.'

'Some of it.'

He sat a cup of coffee in front of me, and next to it a carton of cream which he took from the refrigerator. 'Sugar?'

'No, this is fine,' I said, pouring a little cream into the coffee. 'And when you say about what happened, you mean about the girl, I suppose? I was sorry to hear about, uh, Laurie, was that her name?'

'Yes, Laurie,' he said. 'Laura Rainey. She's dead.'

'So I heard.'

'They think I killed her, but I didn't. I swear to you, I didn't. I would never have harmed her. Not Laurie.'

'I believe you.'

'I wish the sheriff did. It's tough, knowing that he thinks . . . thinks that I did it.'

'Did you love her very much?'

'I . . . ' he started to say, and choked on the words. 'We were just friends, that was all,' he said.

My eyes went involuntarily around the trailer's limited space. He must have seen my puzzlement. There is not a lot of room in a small trailer.

'There's a bed in the back,' he said. 'It's sort of a bedroom back at that end. She slept there. I slept where you are.' Again I must have looked puzzled. 'The dinette makes into a bed,' he said in the way of an explanation.

'Well, it's none of my affair, of course, where either of you slept. And you can tell me to mind my own business if you like, but I really would like to know what happened. Your version of it, I mean.'

'Actually, it'd be good to talk to someone,' he said. 'Someone who isn't so invested in the whole story, if you know

47

what I mean. Mom, Sarah, Anabelle — if I say anything to them about what happened, they start insisting that they know I'm innocent, like they don't even want to hear my side of things. Well Mom, as soon as I start, turns on the waterworks. That's even worse.'

'She's just being a mother. And if you want to talk to me, well, I'm a good listener, and I promise, no waterworks. Or not. It's your call.'

'The trouble is,' he stammered, 'I don't . . . I just don't even know where to begin.'

'Well, you could start by telling me how you and a girl who you say wasn't your lover ended up living together in a small trailer. I take it you mean you were roomies, yes?'

'Yes. Well, mostly we were friends, good friends. Longtime friends. It's kind of hard to explain. You'd have to know Laurie to get it.'

'Okay, then tell me this, which I think is the most important thing: was she a nice person?'

'The best. She was the kindest, sweetest

girl I've ever known, honestly, but . . . '
He hesitated.

'But there was something not quite right about her? Is that what you mean?'

'She was a trollop.' He almost spit those words out.

5

My mouth must have fallen open when he said that. I know I stared wide-eyed at him. 'She was promiscuous, is what you're telling me?'

'Hah!' He snorted. 'Promiscuous doesn't begin to cover it. They called her Anybody's, the local guys did. Because she'd take care of any of them. Any guy who asked. I don't think some of them even *had* to ask.'

'Was she having actual intercourse with these guys?'

'Not all. A few of them, I guess. But only if they wore protection. That was the only rule she had. Otherwise, it was like in the old song, anything goes.'

'Protection? But that's birth control. I thought Catholics don't believe in birth control. Didn't Sarah tell me she was Catholic?'

'I guess she was. But more when it suited her than as a general rule. Is there such a thing as a sort-of Catholic?'

'Probably more than you might think. I suppose there's a sort-of everything, to be honest. But at least she was sensible. About the intercourse, I mean. Insisting on protection is better than leaving things up to chance, I should say.'

'I'd say you were right, except that it wasn't a matter of being sensible, though. Not with Laurie. She just said, whenever the subject came up, that the world was a rotten place, too rotten to bring a baby into it. That was why she didn't want to chance getting pregnant.'

'You know, it sounds to me like she must have been a very unhappy young woman.'

'She was. It started, I think, with her old man. Her father. She didn't want to talk about that, but that was the impression I got from what she did say. He was a bum. He left them, her and her mother, when Laurie was a kid, maybe ten or twelve. She was always vague about that. He just up and disappeared, though. Left for work one morning, as I understand it, and that was the end of that.'

'And he never came back? Or even tried to get in touch?'

He shook his head. 'Not a peep out of him, ever, from what she said. They think he had a girlfriend, and ran off with her. Anyway, as near as I could figure out, that was when it started, her trouble. Maybe she was just looking for him in all those other guys. I don't know. I'm not a psychiatrist, but that's how it always seemed to me.'

'How old was she when she moved in here?'

'She had just turned eighteen. I only know that because she had just had a birthday. She said she was finally old enough to get away from her mother. They hated one another, apparently. She always said they did. And I believed her. Anyway, she never had anything good to say about her mother, not a single word of praise or affection in all the time I knew her.'

'Which might explain why the father left.'

'Probably. So they had this big ruckus,

Laurie and her mom. I don't know exactly what it was about. I doubt that either of them did either. To be honest, I think it was just one long ongoing battle between them. And finally Laurie asked me if she could move in here. With me. It was only meant to be a temporary thing, until she could decide what she wanted to do. But I didn't mind. I was happy to have her here. But,' he added in precise tones, 'it was always understood that it wasn't meant to be a boyfriend and girlfriend kind of thing.'

'Just roomies, in other words.'

'Right. And friends. But she . . . we . . . we never did anything, if you know what I mean.'

'I understand.'

'I couldn't have anyway,' he said with a red face. 'If you want to know the truth, not when I knew about all those others, I couldn't. I didn't want to use her, the way everybody else did. I thought maybe if one guy treated her decently, it would make a difference.'

'But you're saying that it didn't?' I asked.

'I guess not. But the funny thing is, I honestly thought it had. For a long time after she moved in here, for weeks I mean, she wouldn't go out at all, except if the two of us went to the store for something, or like that. Or sometimes we'd go for a walk, but always after dark, and never where we might run into anyone else. It took me a while to figure it out: I think she was afraid of running into any of her old tricks. Afraid they'd expect everything to be the same as it used to be. And I honestly don't think she wanted to do those things anymore. I think she was really trying to, you know, clean up her act.'

'So what happened? Are you saying she reverted back to her old habits?'

He took a long time to answer, and when he finally did, it was more like he was talking to himself than to me, almost as if he'd gone into some kind of trance.

'No. She didn't. Not exactly.'

'I don't understand. Either she stayed on the straight and narrow, or she didn't.'

'She did. Until that night, the night it happened.'

'So what was different about that night?' I asked. 'Something must have set things in motion. There's always something.'

It took a moment for him to answer, and when he did, I again had the impression that he was talking more to himself than to me. He might almost have forgotten that I was there.

'We'd gone for a walk,' he said. 'I told you we did, sometimes, at night.'

'But not where she might run into any of those guys from her past.'

'Right. Well, that night we walked to the park, that little one that runs alongside the lake.'

'I remember that,' I said. 'It wasn't much of a park, just a beach, and not a very good beach either, because there were all those rocks in the ground.'

He nodded. 'That's the one. We stopped to sit on a bench there.'

'Yes, I remember there were benches.'

'Only a couple. And we sat down on one of them, where we could watch the water. For a long time we weren't even talking, we were just sitting there. It was nice, to tell you the truth. It was like, well, like a guy and his girl, if that makes any sense, just being together.'

'Sometimes those are the sweetest moments of all,' I said, remembering times of my own.

'Exactly. It was sweet, maybe the sweetest few minutes we'd spent together since she moved in.'

'But something happened to change everything. What was it?'

He gave me a dark look. 'What happened was, out of the blue, she asked me if I'd kiss her.'

'Did you?'

He had begun to pace the floor in an ever-widening circle and to speak more rapidly, his voice becoming more and more agitated with each step. He seemed to be reliving that fateful night.

'Of course I did. The funny thing was, for years everyone thought we were, you know, sweethearts, but I'd never even kissed her before. Not once. So when she asked me that, of course I did.'

'But it didn't turn out the way you thought?'

'No. I thought it'd be wonderful, like a dream come true, sort of.'

'So what was wrong with it?'

'As it turned out, it wasn't just a kiss she wanted. Not an innocent peck, I mean, which was what I thought she meant when she first asked me. Heck, I even started to kiss her on the cheek, like a friend would, but she turned her head and I ended up kissing her on the mouth, which was apparently what she had in mind. And it was, well, you know, a serious kind of kiss, with her tongue and everything.'

I thought I was beginning to understand. 'And you got turned on.'

'Yes, it's true, I was excited. Why wouldn't I be? Only, she kept trying to get something more going, and I . . . I responded to that, too. Oh, crap, of course I wanted to, only I didn't either, if that makes any sense.'

'I think it does.'

'It was just . . . it felt wrong, it felt, I don't know, it felt somehow like it was dirty. But when I tried to push her away, like it had gone too far, she started crying.'

I could see what an agony this must have been for him, wanting her and not wanting her at one and the same time. He had been at war with himself, with the desires she had awakened in him. A flesh and blood boy, trying to be an angel of good.

'I stood up,' he went on, speaking faster and faster now, the words spilling out of him in a rush, like water over the dam. 'I told her I was going home. She could go or stay, it didn't matter to me. Only she got up too. She was clinging to me, begging me not to go, to let her . . . to let her . . . I can't even say it. But I wouldn't do it either. I couldn't. We must have looked goofy. We were like, dancing around in circles, I was trying to go and she was hanging on to me. She was crying the whole time, too. It was like, oh, man, it plain broke my heart.

'Finally — I don't even know how long this had gone on, maybe a minute or two, not very long — I gave her a shove, hard. It wasn't like I was trying to hurt her or anything like that, I swear I wasn't. I just wanted to get away before things went any further, before they got out of hand. But when I shoved her, she fell to the ground. I guess that's when she hit her head. And I walked away.'

'And she died.'

He cringed, as if I had struck him. 'Yes, she died. But I swear to you, Beth,' he said, his eyes filling up with tears, 'she was still alive when I left her. She was crying, and she called my name, begging me not to go, and I just kept walking away. I left her there, on the ground. If I'd just gone back when she called my name, if I'd only tried to help her, she might still be alive.'

6

He began to cry then. He dropped his face into his hands and his thin young shoulders shook with the force of his sobs.

'I walked away, I left her there,' he cried. 'And I never saw her again. Not alive. They took me to see her at the morgue after she was dead. It was too late then to tell her how sorry I was. If you want to know, the worst thing was I could barely recognize her. That was why they took me to see her, they said, to identify her; but all I could really identify was her clothes.'

'Mike, don't,' I said, and jumping up, I put my arms around him. 'You were trying to do the right thing. Sometimes things just go bad, no matter how hard we try to make them right. It wasn't your fault.'

'But whose fault was it?' he asked through his tears. 'Because someone killed her after I'd gone. It wasn't me, I swear it. But no one believes me. My sisters, my mother, they all say they do, but I can see the truth in their eyes. In their hearts they think the same as the sheriff does. They think I killed her.'

'No, I'm sure they don't,' I cried; but the truth was, I was not altogether sure. They had been so quick to defend him to me earlier, but had they been too quick, too adamant? Maybe he was right. There had been something mechanical in their defense of him. I was sure Sarah thought he was innocent. But Anabelle? And his mother? Looking back, I had my doubts about both of them.

At least his sobs had stopped. He pulled away from me and swiped one sleeved arm across his nose. 'Sorry,' he said. 'You just get here and I start wailing like a banshee. You must think I'm some kind of baby.'

'It's okay. I wish I could do something.'

'You can't,' he said, and his voice was filled with despair.

'Look, do you want me to stay here with you tonight? I can do that, at least, if you need the company. You can even have the bed, and I'll take the dinette.'

He pulled away from me then, and straightened his shoulders. 'No, I'm fine,' he said, sniffling. 'I am, really. To be honest, and don't take offense, please, but just now I think I'd rather be by myself.'

'No offense taken,' I said. 'If you're sure that's what you want.'

'I'm sure,' he said.

'Well, then, it's off to the Lodge for me.' I glanced out the window. 'Oh, shoot, it's raining again.'

'Do you want me to phone Sarah to come and get you?' he asked. 'Or we have a cab company now, just like the big city. To be honest, it's just one guy and his car, but I can call him if you'd like me to. This time of day, he's probably at home. Which means it'll take a while, though, before he shows up. Half an hour, at least. Maybe longer.'

'By which time I'll be snug in my room back at the Lodge,' I said. 'And it's not really raining, nothing more than a few sprinkles, it looks like. I'll be fine. And you?'

'Me too,' he said, managing a smile for me. 'And, Beth, thanks. I promise next time I'll keep it together.'

★   ★   ★

Why, I wondered on the walk to the Lodge, had his story moved me so deeply? Because his young friend, Laurie, had been so desperately unhappy? Many people were.

Or was it because in some way I'd seen myself in her? Not the promiscuity; in that we were different. But, though I had not really thought much about it, I too had been unhappy.

I hadn't thought much about it because I had not *let* myself think about it. It was just how life was, I had always thought. But of course, that was not true. Other people lived lives filled with love and joy. Aunt Thelma was not the norm. She had done what she could, but the truth was, it had not been enough. I had needed, had craved, something more. As Laurie Rainey had craved, too. I had responded by going within myself, a loner, until I had met Sarah. She had taken another path. But surely the loneliness, the longing, had been the same.

The rain, no more than a few droplets when I left the trailer, was coming down hard by the time I reached the Lodge. I ran the last few yards, dodging puddles, and took the wide wooden steps two at a time to the covered veranda that ran all the way around the building.

There, sheltered from the rain, I paused for a minute or two to get my breath back. I could see the lake from here. The wind was up, whipping the waves to a froth. White-topped, they raced in a line like dancers onto the shore, spilling themselves there, to be followed by another row and another, endlessly.

For an eerie moment, standing in the darkness, I thought I heard them: the ghosts of the lake, calling to me on the howling wind. Lost souls drowned long ago, but still restless, still seeking salvation. Perhaps the same salvation that I had sought all my life. Or was it only that one lost soul I heard: the soul of an unhappy young woman begging to be saved, dying an ignominious death instead, alone on a lonely stretch of rocky beach? The skin at the back of my neck felt like it was crawling. I could almost fancy I saw her, reaching out to me, imploring me.

'You're being a goose,' I told myself and, pushing the hood of my poncho back, I went inside. The lights in the lobby were bright and welcoming. A fire burned in an enormous hearth on the far wall, the flames dancing as a moment before the waves had danced.

'You must be Miss Nolan,' a voice said, and a little dumpling of a woman came into the lobby from behind a registration counter. She was short and white-haired and wearing a checked dress, with a dainty little apron tied about her middle. She regarded me over the tops of the spectacles she wore.

'I am,' I replied. 'I'm afraid I am a bit late, though.'

'Never you mind about that. I'm Mrs. Gershon,' she said. 'I'm the proprietress here.'

'Sarah Gladstone was going to drop off

my bag,' I said. 'I hope she remembered.'

'She did, and I've taken it upstairs already, to your room. But before you go up, come into the dining room and have a bite to eat.'

She led the way into the dining room, just off the lobby, pausing at the door to flick on the bright overhead lights. 'I'm afraid you'll have the place all to yourself at this hour,' she said. 'There were some others earlier, locals mostly, the ones who don't like to cook for themselves, so they come here and let me cook for them. Which I don't mind at all. It makes me happy to feed people. Of course, they've all come and gone by this time, but Sarah said you'd be hungry when you came in, so I kept some seafood chowder for you. I hope that's all right for your dinner. It's not at all fancy, but you'll find it filling. And there's plenty of fresh bread; that should still be warm, I think. And afterward, a big slice of apple pie. Homemade. I made the pies myself, from our own apples, right off that tree out front. And after you have some food in you, then I'll take you straight up to your room. It's just on the second floor, not much of a walk. I lit a fire there, too, when I took your bag up, so the room should be nice and toasty for you by now.'

She sat me at a table big enough for a family and went away, returning in just a few minutes to set a huge bowl of steaming fish chowder in front of me, and a plate with a heel of bread (yes, still warm) with a mountain of butter to slather on it. By the time I had wolfed that down, not realizing how hungry I was until I had started eating, she was back with the promised apple pie, an enormous slice with a scoop of vanilla ice cream melting atop its surface. Still later, she did, as promised, show me to my room.

She was very kind and hospitable, and the room was lovely, everything that one might hope for in a country inn. I had every reason to be blissfully content. Still, as I lay under the warmth of a thick obviously handmade quilt, with a fire burning across the room, it was not the flames but the shadows that I watched.

I seemed to see in them a young couple

struggling together. She fell to the ground, and the boy rushed away. Even when I fell asleep, though, as I did soon enough, I could still hear her anguished cry. But perhaps it was only the wind that I heard, still blowing hard from the lake and making the shutters creak and rattle.

Or maybe it was the lost souls of Ghost Lake, crying on the wind to be saved.

7

By morning, last night's storm had blown itself out. I stood at the window of my room and looked out over a lake as serene and smooth as a polished slate. The distant reflection of the morning sunlight on its gray-green surface was so bright as to hurt the eyes, until I had to look away.

I had barely finished my start-of-the-day bathroom routine when the phone by my bed rang.

'There's a diner in downtown Lake Caspar,' Sarah said when I answered, 'where they manage to get your eggs perfect no matter how you order them, and the bacon is shatteringly crisp.'

'I'm in,' I said. 'Give me half an hour to dress and then you can pick me up out front.'

By the time I had dressed and come downstairs, I could see her car waiting in the driveway. Mrs. Gershon was behind the registration counter as I hurried across the lobby. I waved to her as I went.

'Will you be having dinner with us tonight?' she called after me. 'I'm roasting a chicken.'

'Sounds wonderful,' I called back. 'Put me on the list, and thanks.'

* * *

The restaurant Sarah took me to was everything one could hope for in an old-fashioned small-town diner. My eggs were indeed cooked just the way I liked them: whites set with a mere hint of brown about the edges, and the yolks still runny. And the bacon, as promised, was 'shatteringly crisp.' This was an old joke from our school days: Sarah had always insisted that if properly cooked, a rasher of bacon held three inches above your plate and dropped should shatter upon impact. This did. I tested it to be sure, to our mutual amusement.

'Sarah,' I said, cleaning up the crumbles of shattered bacon, 'it's so good to be together again. I'm glad I came.'

'Me too,' she said, beaming.

While we lingered over coffee, I brought her up to date on my brief visit the evening before with Mike. 'I wish there were something I could do to help him,' I finished my story.

'But there is, Beth,' she said. 'That is, if you're up for it.'

'I am. Of course I am. You know me.' At school, what mischief one of us did not dream up, the other had. I had understood Mike's comment the night before about detention, because I had spent so much of my school year in it. 'But what exactly did you have in mind?'

'You work at a law firm, don't you?' She gave me a serious look.

'Yes, Bachman and Bachman,' I said. 'Brothers, those two. But I'm only a lowly secretary there.'

'Hmm.' I could see she was thinking hard.

'Sarah,' I said, 'I don't think I much like that look. Usually when you got that look back in our school days, I was the one who got into trouble. What are you contemplating?'

'I'm just thinking. Do you happen to have a business card with you?' she asked. 'From the law firm?'

'Of course. I always carry them, in case anyone needs a referral.' She put out a hand, palm up. I looked in my purse and found a card, and placed it in the upturned palm. She looked at it for a long moment before thrusting it into the pocket of her blouse.

'Let's go pay the local sheriff a visit,' she said, pushing her cup aside.

'I'd like that, actually. I'd like to hear his side of things. But, you know, apart from just plain old fibbing, which I'm not fond of doing, I think it's probably against the law to pretend you have a license to practice law if you don't. I'm saying, just in case that's what you had in mind.'

'I understand that,' she said. 'And no one's saying you should pretend anything. But if he doesn't ask, then you aren't telling any fibs, are you?'

'That's true enough. But what if he does ask?'

'Then you tell him the truth, that's all.

If there are going to be any dark stains on your soul, I won't be responsible for them. Come on, now.'

★ ★ ★

Of course, it did not take the local sheriff, a middle-aged and somewhat stocky but kindly-looking man, more than a minute or two to ask that question.

'Miss Nolan is with the law firm of Bachman and Bachman,' Sarah introduced me when we were first ushered into his office, handing the firm's card across the desk to him with a flourish.

The sheriff, standing when we came in, studied the card for a few seconds and looked across the neat surface of his desk at me. 'Are you an attorney with the firm, Miss Nolan?' he asked. He glanced again at the card. 'At Bachman and Bachman.'

Just like that, I was busted. I dropped my eyes and said in a very small voice, 'Not exactly.'

'What exactly are you, then?' he asked.

I could feel my cheeks burning. 'A secretary,' I said, and hastily amended, 'A legal secretary, that is.'

'I see.' That was all he said for several minutes. He continued to study the card while I stood across the desk from him and suffered the tortures of the damned. Finally, he raised his eyes to mine and said in a gentle voice, 'And you're asking about this case, I presume, so you can decide whether to suggest to your firm that they handle it?'

He was being tactful, of course, and much kinder than I deserved, I thought. 'Something like that,' I mumbled, dropping my eyes. I was too ashamed to meet his gaze.

'I see,' he said again. He came around the desk and went to the door of his office. 'Willis, could you come in here, please,' he called to the room outside.

A moment later a uniformed deputy came in, the type that I usually thought of as a 'good old boy.' He saw Sarah and me and grinned broadly, showing a row of stained teeth punctuated with gaps. 'Howdy,' he greeted us. 'What's up?'

'These young ladies are here to ask about the Rainey death,' the sheriff said.

Deputy Willis blinked. He had, I noticed, large protuberant eyes. 'You mean little Laurie?' he asked.

'Laura Rainey, yes,' the sheriff said. 'I thought maybe you could show them the scene of the crime, and explain to them how you happened to arrest young Mister Gladstone.' To us, he said, 'Deputy Willis was the investigating officer on the case you're looking into. If you have any questions, I'm sure he will be able to answer them for you to your satisfaction.'

He paused and added, 'Which information you can then pass on to your firm, Miss Nolan.'

8

Deputy Willis took us in a sheriff's patrol car to the park and the beach that ran alongside the lake, the one where according to Mike's story Laura Rainey had died. We exited the car and walked for a few yards, where he stopped.

'Right there,' he said, pointing to a large rock at his feet. It lay half-buried in the ground. 'That's where Miss Laurie fell and hit her head. There was blood to be seen on it, but, well . . . ' He looked out over the nearby water. 'At high tide, you see, the water comes up this far. The lake water has pretty well washed everything clean, but the blood was here before. A lot of it. Not just on the rock, see, but on the sand too.'

'How can you be sure it was that particular rock?' I asked him.

'Oh, I'm sure of it. It was that rock there, all right. You can take my word for that.'

76

I looked around the park. 'There are an awful lot of rocks,' I said somewhat hesitantly. I was groping for anything to undermine his story, the way I had heard our attorneys do in court. But so far I was having no luck. Deputy Willis looked like a dumb yokel, but he sounded pretty sure of his facts.

'This is true,' he said, nodding. 'And there's not a lot of sand. Not now, leastways. It used to be that every spring, before the season started, the town would go and buy sand. That was back when the town had a season to speak of, which they don't so much anymore. Back then, though, they would have the sand trucked in early every spring and spread it around here, to make it more like a real beach. Most of the rocks were buried then, under that new sand. They brought it in from Florida, as I recall. And every winter, when the water was up, which it is in the winter, then the tides would come in and carry off the sand. It was like a war, sort of, the town sanding the beach and the lake taking it away. Happened over and over.'

'You have to understand, though, it's different over where we are,' Sarah said to me. 'Where the lake backs up to our house, the water is plenty deep and generally stays that way unless there's a long drought, and the lake shrinks all over. But there are places near the shoreline, along here, for instance, where sandbars build up. They pose a hazard to boaters. What's even worse, they're movable sandbars, so it's impossible for the lake patrol to chart them like they do other hazards. One time the sandbars are in one location, and the next week someplace else, depending upon the currents. You have to know how to spot them, from the way the water moves over them. Once you've got the knack, though, you can see them at a glance.'

'But not at night,' I said.

'No, not at night. But I don't go out at night,' she said.

'Do you suppose that's what happened to that old ferryboat? The one that sank?'

'No, that wasn't all that far from here, actually, but it had nothing to do with sandbars. It was a car going through the hull that caused that. They brought the boat up a couple of years ago. I remember standing on the town pier with my mother when they towed it in, and you could see the opening for yourself. I was surprised when I saw it that it took as long as it did for the boat to sink.'

'Course,' Willis said, still following his own train of thought, 'they don't haul the sand in anymore like they used to do. It costs too much, and the town's gotten too poor.' He looked at me. 'But never you worry, miss. I'm sure about that rock. It was this one. I would swear to that.'

'How can you be so sure?' I asked.

He looked a trifle embarrassed. 'Well, it looks kind of like a horse, don't you see? The shape of it, I mean.'

'It does?' I stared at the rock, which looked nothing at all like a horse, so far as I could see.

'Why sure it does. There's the head, see,' he said, pointing. 'And the tail, and . . . well, I guess you have to use a little imagination, of course.'

'Of course.' A lot of imagination, I was thinking.

'Anyway, that's what it looks like to me. That's how come I know for certain that it was this rock. It's the only horse rock on the beach.'

I was prepared to accept that this was the rock he had seen earlier, horse-shaped or not. So far I was batting zero. 'The boy says she was alive when he left,' I said, however. 'He swears he's innocent.'

'Well, you know, the prisons are crowded full of innocent men,' Willis said. 'You ask 'em, and every one of 'em will say they shouldn't be there because some witness lied, or their attorney screwed something up, or the judge had something against them. There's always some 'because' or another that's their excuse for being there.'

'But if there are no witnesses to that night, how can you know what happened?'

'But there was,' Willis said in a triumphant voice. 'There was a witness. Old Miss Gibbons, it was. She lives just over there.' He pointed at the nearest house to us, no more than forty feet away.

'You're saying she saw everything?'

'Well, not quite everything. She happened to look out her front window.'

'Happened? Oh, right. Like it was pure chance. I know that woman, Willis. She's the town gossip,' Sarah said.

Willis had the good graces to laugh. 'She does like to keep an eye on what everybody else does, that's the truth,' he admitted. 'But I got to say, she'd have no reason that I can think of to lie about what she says she saw that night.'

'What does she say she saw?'

He took a moment to pull a tin of tobacco out of his back pocket and open it. He tore off a sizable wad and stuffed it into his mouth. 'Well,' he said, speaking around his chew, 'she says for starters they was on that bench, the boy and the girl. That bench, right there.' He pointed. 'And they was spoonin' when she first looked out her window and saw them. Kissing, you know.'

'I know what spooning means,' I told him.

'Oh, sure. It's just, well, we had a speaker came to talk to us at the station a few months back, he said the big problem for police departments these days is communication with the public. I just wanted to be sure we were on the same wavelength, the two of us.'

'Yes. So go on — they were on the bench there, kissing. Or spooning, if you prefer. Please continue.'

'Well, then they both jumped up, she says, and for a minute or two she thought they was dancing, before she caught on that they were fighting. Understand, she could see them, but she didn't hear what they was saying.'

'I understand that.'

'So from what she saw, she thought maybe he was trying to get the girl to do something she didn't want to do. You know what fellas can be like.'

'I do indeed,' I said.

He smiled and nodded. 'And then, for whatever reason, I guess she must have said something he didn't like or whatever, and he pushed the girl, and down she went.'

'And hit the rock.'

'Right. That one.' Again, he pointed. 'Only, that was all Miss Gibbons saw. She closed her drapes then.'

'Why did she?' I asked drily. 'It sounds like she was enjoying the show. So why walk out of the theater before intermission, so to speak?'

'Well, she says,' and he hesitated, looking embarrassed, 'she says it was because he was hanging out of his britches.'

'Hanging out? What do you mean, hanging out?'

'She saw his . . . you know, his . . . ' He was having trouble saying the word.

'His what?' I thought I knew, but I had no intention of letting Officer Willis off the hook that easily.

'She saw his tallywhacker,' he said. 'You know what that is?'

'I think I can figure it out. So, your witness, this Mrs . . . '

'Gibbons. Miss Gibbons. She says she saw his tallywhacker, hanging out of his britches while they was fighting. Well, shoot, of course she closed her drapes then. Wouldn't you? You could not expect a decent woman, a good Christian woman, no matter what else you can say about her, to keep watching after she had seen that, seems like to me.'

'No, I guess not,' I conceded.

'Least that is what she told me when I talked to her,' he said. 'But you can ask her about it yourself if you would rather.'

'No, that will not be necessary,' I said. 'I'm sure you're right: there'd be no reason for her to make that up. I don't see how anyone could, frankly.'

'So there you have it,' he said. 'They was having a fight, and he leaves, and later we find her dead, with her head all bashed in. You can see why we arrested him. Seems pretty clear-cut to me.'

'I can see why you'd think that,' I said. I did not add that Miss Gibbons's story agreed in most particulars with what Mike had told me, at least as far as it went. Miss Gibbons might be a horrible snoop, but it sounded like she had only told the officers what she had honestly seen.

The problem was, she had not seen enough. Unfortunately, she had not seen what actually happened to Laura Rainey. Someone had killed her, yes. But after she had closed her drapes. After Mike had walked away. Who had it been? I wondered. Someone had murdered a poor unhappy girl. One of her boyfriends? A rival? Who in the town of Lake Caspar could possibly have had a motive sufficient enough to commit murder for it?

'If there's anything else I can do . . . ' Willis said, glancing in the direction of his patrol car. I had the impression that, having told us everything he knew, he was now impatient to leave.

'I'll let you know if I think of anything more,' I said. 'Come on, Sarah, I'm ready for that boat ride now, ghosts or no ghosts.'

Willis spat a stream of tobacco juice on the ground and, with a tip of his hat, returned to his car. Sarah and I declined the offer of a ride, and instead walked back to hers.

I wanted time to think about what he had told us. Somewhere in all those details there must surely be a clue to what had actually happened to Laura Rainey. I was determined to find it.

9

So we stopped for our bathing suits and spent most of the rest of the day on the water, sometimes riding about and sometimes diving into the water for a quick swim. Sarah dutifully showed me where there was a sandbar, and how I could tell where there was one, and where not. From which I learned not a thing. The surface of the water looked the same to me either way, but I nodded sagely and pretended I understood.

This was probably the only lake I would ever visit, almost surely the only one with sandbars that moved around from location to location, and probably the last time I would ever be here. And in any case, I was highly unlikely to be piloting a boat for any reason, lake or not, so I could not actually get too interested in spotting sandbars.

Later, she dropped me back at the Lodge. I had a nap and a shower, and was down in the dining room in plenty of time to share it with a handful of others, mostly locals, at a guess. The roast chicken was perfect, served with garlic tinged mashed potatoes and a cocotte of braised spinach, and cherry pie this time for dessert.

When I had eaten, and thinking of those two slices of pie, I decided I would go for a walk before I turned in and try to burn off a few calories. The town of Lake Caspar was not very big, and contrary to Anabelle's dire warnings, I doubted that I was in any danger from criminals strolling through it alone.

Only, I soon realized there really was not much of a town to stroll through. There were a mere two blocks to 'downtown.' I passed some touristy kinds of shops, selling T-shirts and postcards and lots of cheap trinkets; a dark movie theater which apparently opened only on weekends and, to judge from the playbill, showed mostly old westerns; the diner, also closed, where we had breakfast hours earlier; and a bar with some honky-tonk music (Hank Williams, I thought) blasting from its open door and no one inside, it appeared, but a lonely-looking bartender, polishing glasses and looking quite bored. He saw me at the door and brightened briefly, flashing me a smile of welcome, but I only shook my head and walked on.

I was almost to the end of the street when I came to a church. A Catholic church, to judge from the stone grotto near the steps holding a crudely painted statue of the Virgin Mary. I paused outside for a moment or two, remembering that Laura Rainey had been at least ostensibly Catholic, and debating with myself, before I mounted the wide stone steps and pushed at the door, half-expecting to find that this too was closed.

Somewhat to my surprise, the door gave, and I entered. Apparently the local priest shared my confidence in the town's propensity for mischief, or lack thereof. These days, in most large cities, the church would have been locked.

There was a multitude of candles burning inside. Someone's prayers, I thought. If I remembered rightly, in a Catholic church you bought candles and lit them for prayers. The flames fluttered and shimmied for a moment in the draft from the open door, before settling down to their steady luminescence. In their pale light I could see a row of apostles, rather poorly painted, marching down either side wall. A worn red carpet led the way down the center aisle to the apse, where a simple wooden altar was backed by a genuinely impressive reredos. A beautiful hanging depicting Christ on the cross was trimmed with enough gold leaf to have outfitted a Spanish castle. It was all the more impressive for its simple, almost primitive, setting. I stood before the altar for several moments, staring at its backdrop.

'Lovely, isn't it?' a voice said behind me.

I turned and saw that though I had not heard him, a priest had entered the nave behind me, and made his way down the worn red carpet. He stood only a few feet away.

'Yes, Father,' I said. 'It's impressive. And surprising, too, if you'll forgive my saying so.'

'You mean, of course, in contrast to the rest of our lowly church. Yes, you're right. It was a gift from one of our wealthier members. I'm afraid it makes everything else look a bit tawdry. I've wondered often I should take it down, but to be honest, I've never had the heart to do so.'

'I don't think I could either,' I admitted. 'It is beautiful.'

'And people do need beauty in their lives. There's so little else.' He stood with his hands folded before him, contemplating me in a not unfriendly way. 'You're a stranger in our little village, I believe,' he said after a moment.

'Yes. I'm here visiting a friend. Sarah Gladstone. Do you know her?'

'I know the name, certainly.' He almost, but not quite, smiled when he said this.

I felt sure I understood that not-quite smile. 'Yes. I suppose everyone does, small towns being what they are. News gets around.'

'You must be referring to her brother. Michael, isn't it? That seems to be the latest news getting around town.'

'Then you know about that? Michael's incident?'

He gave his head a shake, setting loose a cascade of dark curls. He was actually a handsome young man. I wondered fleetingly how many of his parishioners came to catch sight of him. 'Only a few details,' he said. 'Things people mentioned.'

'It's the sort of thing people *would* mention,' I said.

'It was an unfortunate business.'

'Yes, unfortunate. I wonder, Father, about the girl, Laura Rainey.'

'That was the young lady who died?'

'Yes. I've been told that she was Catholic. Did she come here?'

'For services? Occasionally. Not often, though. I don't think I saw her here more than a half dozen times a year. The big occasions, of course; Christmas, Easter. The occasional Sunday or two. Why do you ask?'

'Did she come here for confession?'

'I'm sure you know that my vows forbid me to discuss her confession with you,' he said, 'or lack of confession.'

For some reason his comment annoyed me, although I did know it was true. 'Yes, I do know that. But I know as well, Father, that a very unhappy young woman is dead now. I'd like to think that before she died her lonely death, someone at least tried to offer her some . . . ' But I hesitated, not sure exactly what I wanted to say. 'Some comfort,' I finished a bit lamely.

'There is comfort to be found in the blood of the lamb,' he said, assuming a pious expression.

'That's kind of a stock answer, isn't it?' I replied quickly.

'Maybe, but it's true.'

'With all due respect, I think, Father, she would have been glad for something a little closer to earth.'

'By which, you mean . . . ' He raised one eyebrow.

'Some human comfort. Maybe simply someone to hold her, without any ulterior motive. I think maybe she needed that; needed it desperately. I think that may even be why she's dead now.'

'Or maybe she died for her sins,' he suggested.

'Yes, maybe. Good night, Father,' I said abruptly. I had had enough piety for one evening.

I went past him then, following that worn red carpet back to the entryway. As I pushed the door open — rather angrily, I admit — I looked back to find the priest staring after me with that same beatific smile on his face.

That, I thought, was probably as much comfort as he had ever given that poor girl. As much, it would seem, as she had gotten from anyone.

On my way back to the Lodge, I saw Deputy Willis drive slowly by in his patrol car, glancing my way as he passed. So they were keeping an eye on me, were they? Fine, I thought, still angry from my encounter with the young priest. It just meant I did not have to worry about Anabelle's criminals. Though to be frank, I wondered why Anabelle should have to worry about them. She was rather formidable. Too formidable, I thought, to be mistaken for vulnerable.

10

I was curious to meet Laura Rainey's mother, she about whom Laura had had no good words to say, according to Mike. I may have met her when I was here as a child, but if I had, I had kept no memory of that. So the following day over breakfast (at the diner, again), I asked Sarah where to find her.

'We used to live right next door,' she said. 'Which is the place you remember from before.'

'Would I have met her then?'

'It's possible, but not likely. We weren't on neighborly terms. My mother thought she was crass. Anyway, we lived next door, but we didn't socialize. This was just after Daddy left, and before he died. Things were tight for us then, and that was a much cheaper neighborhood. But Mom was still the beneficiary on the insurance; he hadn't changed that, for whatever reason. I suspect he just plain forgot. And when Daddy died in that car crash, which was only a couple of years later, she got all the money. Much to her surprise. So we moved up in the world. To a new house, the one where we are now.'

'And your mother treated herself to *the ring*.'

'That too,' Sarah admitted.

'So this cheaper neighborhood you lived in back then — I've forgotten where it was, exactly. Not right on the lake, as I remember.'

'Property on the lake, even a small house like ours, is expensive.'

'The old place, is it far?'

'Not very. If you follow the lake road, the old one, west out of town, you'll come to a market alongside the road. It's more of a farmer's stand, really. That's Apple Harvest Drive. Take a left there. Well, that's the only direction you can go, unless you want to drive into the lake. Our house was the one smack dab at the very end of the road, the pink one. It looks like you're going to drive right in the front door if you don't stop. Elvira Rainey's house was the one next to ours.

It's wood, and it was once painted white, but the last I saw there wasn't much paint to be discerned. But last time I was out that way, they were the only two houses there, so I don't think it should be too hard to find them. There was another one, past ours a little, but it burned down some years ago. Vandals, they think. Or hippie squatters.'

'Sounds like I'll need to rent a car, then, I suppose.'

'No, don't. You can use mine. I can always borrow Mom's if I need to. In a pinch, I might even coax Anabelle to drive me somewhere. Or, as you say, the town isn't that big. I can walk almost anywhere I'd need to go.'

*   *   *

Their house, the old one, had been empty for years. I had only the vaguest memory of coming here before, and memory had convinced me it was bigger than it was in reality. I wondered that Mrs. Gladstone had not long ago sold it. Maybe there had been some fantasy of her husband returning to it, though surely that dream had died as well in that auto crash that took his life and made her fortune.

Of course, this was not the most desirable of locations. There was only this house and the one next door, obviously the Raineys'. Otherwise, Apple Harvest Drive, for its grand name, was really nothing more than a dirt and gravel track, heavily rutted, that cut through, yes, an apple orchard.

After the orchard, it crossed some train tracks. (Did I remember from before the noise of a train passing, tooting its whistle? I thought I did.) Beyond the tracks, the road made a sharp bend to the left, after which it ran for a mile or so through some fields where nothing grew now but weeds, though I thought I recalled corn. But how would anybody know what they really remembered and what they only wanted to remember? The facts, as opposed to their opinions? Some people said your past shaped your present, but it was the other way around, wasn't it? Your past was informed by your present, shaped by it, wasn't it?

And there, at the end of the road — it seemed to appear all of a sudden — was the house. As Sarah had said, it sat smack dab in front of me, as if I could drive right in through the front door. As, now that I saw it, I remembered. Except I had remembered it as much larger, and I could see now that it was tiny. Not as tiny, however, as the house in which I had grown up, Aunt Thelma's house.

And yes, as Sarah had said, beyond that empty house where the Gladstones had once lived were some charred remains of another, the one that had burned. Mrs. Rainey — Elvira, Sarah had called her — lived in the other house remaining on the track; the one that, so Sarah said, had once been painted white, though there was no evidence now to be seen of white paint. And Mrs. Rainey was who I had come to see.

Except, when I approached it now, the Rainey house had that same unlived-in look as the Gladstones' former home. A shutter hung loose at a front window, and one of the three wooden steps leading up to the door was broken in, so that I was obliged to take a giant step from the first to the last.

I knocked on the door without much hope, and was about to leave when the piece of tablecloth hanging inside as a curtain over the window in the door slid to the side an inch or two, not enough to let me see in, but presumably enough for someone inside to see out. It stayed there for a long minute or two, which I suppose meant someone was looking me over. Then it dropped back into place, and after a moment the door opened, but only a sliver.

'You're not from the welfare people, are you?' a voice asked.

'No, I . . . I'd like to talk to you a minute, though, if I can,' I said. I was so prepared to be disappointed, I had not actually planned what to say if I did find the woman.

My reply seemed to satisfy her, however. She closed the door and I heard a safety chain rattling inside before she opened it again, this time wide enough to let me pass through.

Having done so, however, I was not

sure if I should be grateful for being permitted to enter or not. To put it as nicely as possible, the room into which I stepped was a pig sty. Ashtrays overflowed with cigarette butts; unwashed dishes, some of them actually covered with mold, crowded every table surface; and glasses, some empty, some half-full, sat with the dishes. The linoleum floor looked as if it had not been swept in months, and there was dust everywhere. The placed reeked of the smell of rotten food, so much so that I had to force myself not to gag.

'They're always trying to catch me at something,' she said, finding a longish stub of a cigarette in one of the ashtrays. She took a large wooden kitchen match from the pocket of the flannel shirt she wore and striking it across a door frame, lit the half smoked stub. 'Those welfare people I'm talking about. I've taken to pretending I'm not home when they come around snooping. Now, who did you say you were again?'

'I didn't. I'm Beth Nolan, a friend of the Gladstones. They used to be your neighbors, just across the way there.'

'Gladstones?' She puzzled over that for a moment. Then her face went dark and her eyes narrowed. 'You're not talking about that boy, are you? The one that killed my little girl?'

'Mike, yes, those Gladstones. But he says he didn't. He did not kill your daughter.'

'Huh. He coaxed her away from her mother, wanted her to come live with him in some little trailer he had, when she had a real home here, and now she's dead, ain't she? I'd call that as good as killing her, whatever he says.' She shoved the cigarette end back in the ashtray where she had found it, stabbing it out. 'Say, you wouldn't happen to have a cigarette on you, would you, dearie?' she asked.

'I'm afraid not,' I apologized. 'I don't smoke.'

'That's too bad. About you not having one, I mean. It's probably better for you if you don't, though. You never did?' I shook my head.

'Good for you, I'd say. As for that other business, I have nothing to say to you about that. I don't care what anybody says, Laurie was a good little girl till that boy got hold of her. Oh, she was sort of rambunctious sometimes, I suppose. What teenager isn't, I'd like to know. I intended to tell the cops that, too, if they had ever come to ask me anything.'

Which surprised me. 'They didn't?' I asked. 'I mean, they didn't come to talk to you? Not at all?'

'Well, they wouldn't I guess, would they? She hadn't lived here in the longest time, maybe half a year, or longer. Anyway, they had that boy right off, the one people say killed her. Don't imagine her body was even cold before they had him in custody. What would they need to talk to me about? What could I tell them that they didn't already know?'

I looked about the tawdry room, a glimmer of hope springing to life in my mind. 'Did she have her own room here, Laurie?' I asked.

She gave me a scornful look. 'Of course she did. Like I said, she was a teen. You know what they're like, I imagine. They always think they need a space of their own, don't they?'

'Then if the police didn't come here after she died, they mustn't have searched her room.'

'How could they, if they weren't here?' she asked.

'Could I? If you wouldn't mind.'

'What? Look at her room, you mean? I don't see why not. It's just down that hall there, to the back. But if you find any money while you're in there, it's mine.' She laughed mirthlessly for a few seconds. 'That's a joke, dearie. She wouldn't have had any money. Not that girl. She never did, far as I knew. Go ahead, look at it if you want. Won't bother me any. Just leave things as you find 'em, is all I ask.'

'Thank you, I will.'

I started down the hallway toward the rear of the house, but she called after me, 'No joke, though — if you do find any money in there, it's mine.'

11

The door at the end of the hallway was closed, but not locked. I no sooner entered Laurie's room than I immediately noticed one major difference. Or, rather, I smelled it. The scent of lemon oil. There was a coating of dust everywhere, of course, and the room smelled like one that had been long closed up; but unlike the rest of the house, this room was neat and tidy, and it had obviously been kept clean when she was still here. It made me automatically feel better about the young woman who had once lived here.

But apart from that, it did not seem that there were any clues to be found that might explain her death. Everything was in its place. This, apparently, was not a girl to leave things uncared for.

The windows were all closed. I supposed they had been since Laurie left, and the air was decidedly stale. I went to one of the windows and, unlocking it, opened it a few inches. A welcome gust of air swept in. I breathed it in gratefully.

I thought, opening the drawer of a nightstand and discovering a cell phone there under some magazines, that maybe I had been too hasty in thinking there was nothing to be found here. I powered up the phone, and at once found myself staring at a photo, taken with the phone, of a man in what could only be described as a compromising position. He was seated in a chair, his pants in a gray-brown puddle at his feet, and he was, to put it nicely, aroused.

Unfortunately, he was also faceless. Whoever had taken the picture, presumably Laura Rainey, had shot him from the neck down. One supposed that in doing so, she had both protected his identity and preserved for posterity what she considered his essential qualities.

I scrolled through the rest of the photos stored in the phone, but found nothing else of interest: wildflowers, some views of the lake, the outside front of a bar. No more nude men, however. Not sure in what way it might be useful to me, I dropped the phone nevertheless into my purse. Apparently Mrs. Rainey was unaware of its existence. I could not see that any harm would be done if she remained so a bit longer. I promised myself that I would return it. In time.

Search though I might, alas, I could find nothing else of interest in the room. After twenty minutes or so of opening and closing drawers, closets, even looking under the twin bed, I gave it up as a lost cause. Whatever Laura Rainey's secrets, they were not to be discovered here — except, of course, for that one salacious picture. I wondered why that was there, and nothing else.

I went back to the main part of the house. Her mother saw me coming down the hall and raised a questioning eyebrow.

'Sorry, I found no money,' I told her. 'Not a penny.'

She shrugged. 'I didn't expect you to. I hope you found whatever you were looking for, at least.'

'No, nothing, but thanks anyway for letting me look.' The phone in my purse felt as if it weighed a ton. For a moment,

I even thought by rights I should hand it to her. But I decided against it. If nothing else, I wanted to know who that man in the picture was.

'If you care,' she said as I was letting myself out the front door, 'she's being buried this afternoon, at two o'clock. There won't be any funeral. I couldn't afford that. Just the service at the cemetery. Mount Olive, a mile or so out of town. Ask anybody in town, they'll tell you how to find it.'

Had I remembered to close that window? I wondered as I went out. But I could not see that it mattered much. This house was hardly the sort of place a serious burglar would pick to break into, and the fresh air could only be good for things.

Outside, I paused at the car with the door open and looked at the house next door, where the Gladstones had once lived. On an impulse, I reclosed the car door and went there.

As I had expected, the front door was unlocked. But there was even less to be seen here than there had been at the place next door. Clearly no one had lived or even visited here in years. The thick coat of dust on the floor was undisturbed by tracks, neither of wild animal nor of human. I left my own highly visible footprints in it as I went to the kitchen. An old cast-iron stove, probably too heavy and impractical to be moved, was the only furnishing in that room. The cupboard doors stood open, revealing bare shelves. A doorless niche where obviously once a water heater had stood gaped open, revealing its bare pipes.

I went back to the front room and took the stairs that ascended the far wall to the bedrooms above. The stairs grumbled and groaned in protest as I mounted them, but the two bedrooms and the bathroom upstairs were as empty as the downstairs had been, closet doors standing open to reveal their emptiness as well.

On an impulse, I went to the window of what I remembered as the children's bedroom and, using a hanky from my purse to wipe the glass clear of some of the dust, looked out. Yes, as I thought, it overlooked the Rainey residence. Had young Mike stood years earlier at this very window and fantasized about the girl he would later be accused of killing?

On an impulse, I looked up. A hill rose up behind the two houses, and there was a man at the top of it, sitting astride a motorcycle. The distance was too great and the sun was in my eyes, so I could not really tell much about him. What I saw was more a silhouette than a real sighting. I had the impression that he was watching not me so much as the Rainey house. For what? I wondered.

The motorcycle's engine suddenly roared to life, and a moment later he was gone. Had he seen me at the window looking at him? Impossible to say. Something had spooked him. Or perhaps he had only stopped there by chance to smoke a cigarette, or stretch his legs, and now he had moved on.

I still had that feeling of being watched. I seemed to sense something behind me, and I turned quickly, half-expecting to surprise someone, but there was no one and nothing there, only some dust motes dancing in a beam of sunshine. I leaned against the windowsill and surveyed the empty room, half-waiting to see . . . something. I hardly knew what.

I was too modern, too much of a realist, to believe in ghosts; but it did seem to me that ever since I had come to Lake Caspar, I had indeed been haunted. Not by those silly ghosts of the lake. I could no more believe in them than I did in fairies or goblins.

But I was haunted, certainly, by the ghost of a young woman, unhappy, desperately searching for love and in her despair driving away what had possibly been her one hope of ever finding it. I had always rather thought that many people do the same thing. It is not an uncommon fault. Perhaps I myself had been guilty of it. But surely, not a fault worthy of dying for.

But the sense of being crowded in upon by unseen people, by the ghosts of the past, overwhelmed me. I fled, yes, fled, actually running down the stairs, out of that house, to the waiting car. In it, I took one last look at the hillside beyond, but the motorcycle and its rider were gone.

Perhaps I had only imagined them. Perhaps they too were ghosts.

I started up the engine and drove away as fast as the rutted road would allow. I did not look back as I went.

If anything pursued me down that lonely road, I did not want to see it.

12

It was only a little after eleven by the time I got back to the town of Lake Caspar, still too early for Laura Rainey's two o'clock burial service. I decided to treat myself to lunch at that diner downtown.

Sarah and I usually had breakfast at the counter, but this time, alone, I took a booth. My waitress was there no more than a minute after I sat down, introducing herself as Emily. 'Em,' she said. 'That's what everyone calls me.'

I ordered a burger and fries, and a glass of milk. They came surprisingly soon. Em had brought them and left, when I suddenly became aware of someone standing by my table. At first, I assumed the waitress had just come back to check on me, but when I looked, I saw a sweet-looking gray-haired lady smiling down at me.

'Hello?' I greeted her, puzzled. I did not think I knew her. 'Can I help you?'

'You're that new girl, aren't you?' she asked. 'I just wanted to tell you . . . well, to warn you, actually.'

'Mary,' Em said in a stern voice, walking up quickly, 'you know perfectly well you're not supposed to be in here.'

'Warn me of what?' I asked, but the waitress was hustling Mary away toward the exit door.

'Death,' she managed to shout back at me as she was shoved outside. 'Death is coming for you.' Then she was gone, and the door once again closed.

'Don't worry about her,' Em said, coming back past my table. 'That's just old Mary. Everybody calls her Crazy Mary. Don't let her spoil your lunch.'

'I won't,' I promised. But the truth was, she already had. Death? Whose death? I wondered. Mine?

I pushed what was left of my burger aside. Of course, if she was really crazy, it probably meant nothing. I certainly hoped so. Death? If there was one word guaranteed to spoil your appetite . . .

It was still early when I left the diner. On a whim, I stopped by the downtown strip mall to see Laurie's therapist, a Doctor Welles who, so Sarah had told me, had an office suite a few doors down from the supermarket that anchored the little mall.

I found the office with no difficulty. A printed sign on the front door advertised Therapy and both Individual and Family Counseling, and welcomed walk-ins. The door was unlocked, but the front office was empty when I went in. There was a receptionist's desk before me but no one was at it. I stood for a moment, staring at the empty desk, where I could see a computer screen slowly scrolling through a variety of flowers.

While I stood there, the door to the inner office opened and a man appeared, wearing a shirt with turned-up sleeves and a tie but without the suit's jacket. He held a half-eaten sandwich in one hand.

'Oh, hello,' he greeted me, waving the ham and cheese as if offering it to me. 'I thought I heard someone come in. My secretary's out to lunch and she must have forgotten to lock the door. Did you have an appointment?'

'No, I just stopped on an impulse,' I told him. 'I was hoping you might have a few minutes to spare, though.'

'Well . . . ' He looked regretfully at what remained of the sandwich.

'I won't take long, I promise,' I said.

'I suppose . . . won't you come into my office, Miss . . . ?'

'Nolan. Beth Nolan.'

He ushered me into his inner sanctum and followed me, closing the door to the outer office behind himself. 'What can I help you with, Miss Nolan? Of course, if you were wanting counseling, it would be better if we set up an appointment.'

'No, that won't be necessary. To be honest, I was hoping we might talk about a patient of yours,' I said. I turned, and suddenly froze. The chair behind his desk was an antique, and distinctive, as was the Oriental rug on which it sat. I had seen both chair and rug, in fact, recently: in Laura Rainey's cell phone. I looked back at the doctor. The picture had been faceless, but, yes, the man's general build matched the one in the photo.

'Of course, I can't talk to you about my

clients,' he said. 'Professional ethics. I hope you understand.'

'Oh, I do,' I said, taking a step in his direction. 'Yes, I understand ethics very well, Doctor Welles. You *are* Doctor Welles, I assume.'

'I am,' he said, looking now wary.

'But I can't help wondering,' I said, 'If you understand them. Do you, I wonder?'

He gave me an angry look. 'I don't think I like the sound of that very much. What exactly are you suggesting, if anything? That sounded like an accusation.'

'An accusation? Yes, I suppose it is.'

'Well, then, Miss . . . Miss Nolan, was it? What exactly are you accusing me of?'

'I'm saying, Doctor, that you took advantage of one of your clients by engaging in a sexual relationship with her. A poor, desperately unhappy girl who came to you for help. I think that's probably illegal. It's certainly immoral. I might even say disgusting.'

'I . . . I . . . ' he sputtered. Yes, he actually sputtered. I got droplets of spittle on my face. 'What do you mean? I don't know what you're talking about. What client? What girl, for heaven's sake?'

I took Laura's cell phone out of my purse and opened it to the picture of the naked man sitting in the chair, the same chair standing just now behind his desk, with the same Oriental rug on the floor beneath it.

'That's you, isn't it?' I demanded, holding it up so he could see the picture clearly.

He stared wide-eyed at the image, obviously at a loss for words. Finally, he went behind his desk, tossing the unfinished sandwich into a waste basket, and sank into the very chair in the picture.

'She was supposed to have gotten rid of that,' he said finally. 'She swore to me that she'd taken it off her phone.'

'Perhaps you should feel flattered, Doctor,' I said, not bothering to hide my disdain. 'I suspect that wasn't the only photograph of the sort that she took, but it seems to be the only one she kept. I wonder why that was.' I looked again at the photo. 'I have to say, I don't see anything remarkable.'

He looked up at me, his face ashen, his eyes tortured. 'What are you going to do?' he asked in little more than a whisper.

'Do?' I considered that for a moment. 'I honestly don't know. I hadn't thought that far ahead. I suppose if I reported it, you'd lose your license, wouldn't you? At the very least.'

He nodded, saying nothing.

'And probably you'd be arrested as well.'

'Yes, of course,' he said finally. 'We both know I'm at your mercy. Please — what are you going to do?

'I don't know,' I said. I did not want to tell him that I had only realized his guilt a few minutes earlier, when I had seen his office. Clearly he thought I had come here already knowing the unsavory truth.

'I'll tell you what,' I said. 'Let me think about that for a few days, and I'll get back to you.' A few days, I thought, but did not say, that would surely be a living hell for him, while he stewed about what I might do. And, just at the moment, I honestly had no idea what that might be.

'I . . . please,' he said, or rather, croaked. 'Please, I beg you.'

'Like you begged Laura Rainey?'

'I didn't,' he said. 'I swear it. I can explain.'

'I'd rather you didn't,' I said, cutting him off.

'I only want to say . . . you need to know. It was her idea, not mine. She was the one who begged, not me. She begged me to . . . to do things with her. I told her it was wrong, on every count. I told her how risky it was for me. But she didn't care at all about that. I know she was young, at an age when she ought to have been still innocent. Maybe you think she was, even. But you have no idea how twisted she was by the time she came to me, or how persuasive she could be when she wanted something. She went on and on. And finally, I simply couldn't resist any longer. I did what she wanted.'

'Stop,' I said, holding up my hand. 'I don't want to hear your excuses. Nothing you say could ever justify your actions.'

I swept out of his office, leaving him at his desk with his head in his hands. A young woman, presumably his secretary, was just coming in the front door from outside. She saw me, and paused just inside the room.

'Is the doctor . . . ?' she started to ask.

'I think, just at the moment, the doctor doesn't want to be disturbed,' I told her, and went past her.

I did not say that I thought the doctor was already disturbed enough for one day.

13

By the time I brought Sarah's car to her, it was almost exactly one o'clock. Laura's burial was scheduled for two. I asked Sarah if she would go with me to the cemetery. 'I think if you go, Mike can go too,' I said. 'I think he has to be chaperoned.'

'He does,' she said. 'Me or Mom have to be with him. We put up the bail money when he was initially arrested.'

'I suspect he'd like to be there. If you go, he could go too.'

She agreed. And I was right. Though he showed little emotion, I could see that Mike was delighted to be asked. We were there at the cemetery at two sharp. On the way, I told them about my visit to Doctor Welles and what had transpired.

'Him too?' was all Mike said, but I could see that he had not received the news well. I should have taken that as a warning, but just at the moment I had other things on my mind.

It did not occur to me until we were actually at the cemetery, however, that I should have thought of flowers. One cheap-looking bunch of daisies that had 'supermarket' written all over them sat alone and forlorn-looking by the waiting casket. The casket of course, was closed. She had been beaten to death, as I recalled. Probably the job of reconstructing her face was too great a challenge for the undertakers.

Apart from Mrs. Rainey and we three, and a minister who spoke briefly and vaguely, and the funeral director who sat waiting in his limousine, there was no one else there to start. But as the minister was speaking, mouthing platitudes and generalities, a man in leather rode up on a motorcycle and sat on his bike by the side of the road just behind. I wondered if he had sent the flowers. Looking down the hill at him, I wondered, too, if he was the same man I had seen watching the Rainey house earlier. I had not then gotten a good enough look at him to say for certain, but the way this man sat astride his bike looked familiar.

When the brief service was over, the minister retired to his own car and promptly drove away. Workmen appeared from somewhere nearby, seemingly waiting for us to leave so they could finish their job. And the funeral director got out of his limousine carrying a large umbrella, though it was not raining, and made his way up the hill to where Mrs. Rainey stood by herself next to the closed casket. He held the umbrella over her head solicitously.

It was at this point in time when the leather-clad stranger got off his motorcycle and walked up the slight hill to the gravesite. He stood for a moment staring down at the closed casket, as if he could see the dead girl within. He showed, so far as I could see, no emotion, and stepped back respectfully when the funeral director appeared and the workmen came forward to lower the casket into the ground.

By the time the motorcyclist made his way back down the hill, Sarah, Mike and I had already made our way back to the road and Sarah's waiting car. As the stranger once more mounted his bike, I walked over to him quickly, before he had an opportunity to leave.

'Was it you who sent the flowers?' I asked him. He nodded without speaking. 'I think I saw you earlier, out behind the Rainey house. That was you, wasn't? On the hillside?' Another nod.

He looked beyond me, to Sarah and Mike, standing next to her car. 'That's the boy, isn't it?' he asked. 'The one they say killed her?'

'Mike Gladstone? Yes, it is. And he does say he didn't kill her. Would you like to meet him?'

I think he intended to decline, but I did not wait to give him the opportunity to do so. I waved Mike over immediately. He must have been waiting for just such an invitation, because he was there in a trice, Sarah following him a bit more slowly.

'This gentleman . . . ' I started to say, and hesitated. I said to the cyclist, 'I don't think you gave me your name?'

'Sam,' he mumbled.

'Sam is the one who sent the flowers,' I

told Mike. 'I knew you'd want to thank him.'

'Thanks,' Mike said none too graciously. Sam only nodded once again in acknowledgment. I was beginning to think Sam was not the loquacious sort.

'Were you a friend of Laura's?' I asked him, determined to get some kind of conversation out of him.

'Laura?' He looked puzzled at me.

'The dead girl,' I said. Which, since he had admitted to sending flowers, I would have thought he knew. I would have been mistaken, however.

'Oh. Was that her name? We just called her Anybody's,' Sam said. 'Me and the guys.'

Mike was quick to say, 'Her name was Laura. Laurie to her friends.'

'Really? Well, that's good to know. I'll tell the others.'

'Yes, do,' I said. Of course, since he had also admitted to being outside the Rainey house earlier, he obviously already knew who she was.

If he noticed my sarcasm, however, he showed no sign. 'Well, nice meeting you all,' Sam said. He stood to kick-start his motorcycle.

'Wait, I — ' I started to say, but he turned his bike smartly around in the road, sort of duck-walking it till he was clear of the limousine.

The funeral director returned to his car with Mrs. Rainey on one arm and the umbrella aloft. He opened the rear door of the limousine for her, but before she got inside, she gave me a resentful look.

'You didn't have to tear her room all to pieces,' she said, and disappeared into the car without waiting for a reply.

While I was puzzling over that bit of information, Sam revved up his engine and drove off. The sound of his bike faded slowly in the distance.

★   ★   ★

On the way back into town, I thought of what Mrs. Rainey had said about the room being torn apart. And thinking back, I remembered the window I had maybe left open. Sam must have come back later and, finding an open window, let himself into the house, to search Laura's bedroom.

What had he been searching for? I wondered. Had I missed something in my brief look-through? More pictures, perhaps? If Laura Rainey had taken one of her therapist, she had most likely taken others. Had there been pictures of Sam? And if so, where? In her camera? But I had found only the one incriminating picture in the camera, the one of Doctor Welles. Had there been printed photographs that I simply had not found?

'Just out of curiosity,' I asked the two in the car on the way back into town, 'Bikers always have someplace to hang out together, don't they? Is there any place like that here in Lake Caspar?'

'There's a biker bar, the Eagle's Nest,' Mike said. 'We go past it, in fact, just down the road a bit from here.'

A minute or two later, he pointed to the right. 'There,' he said. 'That's the Eagle's Nest. The biker bar. We're going by it now. Why did you ask about that?'

I turned to look at the bar, and as I did, I saw a familiar rider strolling from his bike in the parking lot toward the bar's front door. *Hello, Sam*, I thought. *Now I know where to find you.*

'Just curious,' I answered Mike.

14

On the way through town, Mike asked if we could drop him off at the supermarket in the little strip mall. 'There's a few things I need to pick up,' he explained.

'Technically, I'm supposed to be with you,' Sarah said. 'Any time you're out of your trailer.'

'I think you'd probably be bored,' he said. 'Walking up and down the aisles with me. You know how I am at a grocery store. I have to look at everything in case there's something I need that I didn't think of. And anyway, realistically, what would be the point? What trouble can I get into at a supermarket?'

'That's true enough, I suppose. Well, okay,' she agreed. 'But, please, don't assault any of the check-out girls while you're there, okay?'

'I promise you they'll be safe,' he said.

We dropped him in the supermarket lot and waited until we had seen him actually go inside the store before we drove off. 'Just to be safe,' as Sarah put it.

As we went through the parking area on our way out, I remembered that Doctor Welles's office was in the very same little mall. I glanced at the storefront as we drove by. I almost pointed out to Sarah that it was only a few doors down from the supermarket. But surely she knew that without my reminding her.

Needless to say, I should have trusted my instincts.

* * *

'Is there anywhere you want to go before I take you back to the Lodge?' Sarah asked when we were back on the road again.

'Yes, I'd like to . . . ' But I hesitated, reluctant to admit what I wanted.

'Oh, dear, that bad?' she said. 'You might as well spit it out. You've got my curiosity aroused now anyway.'

'I'd like to go to that bar,' I said.

'Bar?' She gave me a puzzled look. 'What bar?'

'That biker bar. The one we passed on the way into town. Mike pointed it out.'

'Do you mean the Eagle's Nest? Are you serious? Why on earth would you want to go there?' She looked alarmed by the suggestion.

'If you really want to know, I'd like to talk more with that man, Sam. And that's the only place I know of where I might find him.'

'That's true enough, I guess. But sweetheart, have you ever been to a biker bar?' I shook my head. 'I thought not. They're not for people like us, you know. They're not the most genteel types, the bikers. Their girlfriends can be even tougher than they are. And if there's anything we learned at Miss Parker's, it was how to be ladies. Trust me, these women don't even know the meaning of the word.'

'I suppose you're right. But I still want to go. I *need* to go. I need to talk to him. Will you take me there?' Still, she hesitated. 'Or,' I said, 'it doesn't seem to me like it was very far back. I'm sure I can get there on foot. I'll understand if you don't want to take me. No hard feelings, I promise. Just drop me anywhere along here, is fine.'

'No, there's no need for you to walk,' she said. 'Of course I'll take you if you've got your heart set on going. Besides, you may need your strength. Save it for later, in case you have to run.'

There were several bikes in the parking lot of the Eagle's Nest, but ours was the only car. Sarah drove up right in front of the door and kept the motor running. I was thinking it looked familiar. Of course, I realized — I had seen it in Laurie's phone. This was the bar front she had photographed. Which meant that at some time, for some reason, she must have been here as well.

'Can I buy you a beer?' I asked, one hand on the door handle. After her warnings, I was putting off the moment as long as I could.

'In that place? Thanks, but not a chance,' she said. 'Are you sure you want to go in there yourself?'

'No, I'm not sure, but I'm going

anyway.' I opened the door and got out. 'Well . . . '

'See you, kiddo. And don't say you weren't warned,' she said, and drove smartly out of the lot. Leaving me alone in that parking lot full of motorcycles. It took me a long moment of staring at the door to screw up my courage to go up to it and push it open.

When I first went inside, it was so dark after the bright light outside that I could see almost nothing. I stood just inside the door for a minute or so, blinking furiously. When finally I could see again, it was to discover that I was the center of all attention. The bar was half-full. Mostly men, a few raunchy-looking women. And everyone in the place was staring at me.

'Uh, sugar,' the beefy looking bartender said to me, 'are you sure you're in the right place?'

'Don't mind me, I'm not staying. I'm just looking for someone,' I told him, and looked around. 'Oh, there he is.' I spotted Sam standing in a far corner talking to a trio of tough-looking women dressed in leather, as he was. Sarah was right, they looked tougher than the men in the room. 'Yoo hoo, Sam. Hi,' I called. 'Remember me?'

He said something to the women. Whatever it was, must have been funny. All three laughed heartily. Their eyes stayed on me. They were not friendly.

Sam said something more to them out of the corner of his mouth and sauntered across the bar to where I stood just inside the door. They watched him go with keen interest. So did I. He was smiling as he strode up to me, but his eyes were anything but welcoming. He was clearly angry to see me. He came within inches of me, so close I could smell his body odor. Sweaty. Plus, he had smoked some pot recently. I could smell that too.

'Are you crazy?' he said to me in little more than a hiss. 'They chew up chicks like you in a place like this and roast them for dinner.'

'I needed to talk to you,' I whispered back.

He took a firm grip on my elbow.

'Okay, we talk outside,' he said, and piloted me deftly and none too gently out the door.

15

'Now,' he said when we were back in the sunlight, 'what's so damned important that you'd risk your neck for it by coming here? How did you find me, anyway?'

'I'm entitled to some secrets, aren't I?'

'Huh.' He grunted. 'Didn't anyone ever tell you about bikers?'

'Some.'

'And you weren't scared?'

'No,' I lied.

'Then they didn't tell you enough. Or you're stupid, is all I can say. You should have been scared.'

'Okay, maybe I am, a little scared,' I admitted. 'But I still wanted to talk to you, and where else was I going to find you? It was here and now, or never.'

'Talk to me about what, for crap's sake?' he asked, exasperated.

'That was you, wasn't it? Who searched Laura Rainey's bedroom?'

'What are you talking about?'

'When we were at the cemetery, her mother said her room was all torn up. She accused me of doing it. But it wasn't torn up when I left there. Which means somebody came in after I left. That was you, I'm thinking.'

'What if it was?' He gave me a cagey look.

'What were you looking for?'

'I didn't even say I was there. But what if I was? Why is that any of your business?' he asked in a defensive tone.

'You were looking for pictures, weren't you?'

'What makes you say that?'

I gave him a knowing look.

His eyes narrowed. 'Do you have them?'

I couldn't help a smile. I had just scored a big point. 'So you were looking for photographs? You have as much as admitted it.'

'If I was, I didn't find any.' He hesitated for a moment. 'They'd have been in her phone, if they were there. But I didn't find a phone either.'

'That's because I have it,' I said.

He looked suddenly excited. 'Did you look through it?' I nodded. 'Were there . . . ?' But again he hesitated.

'Pictures of you?' I finished for him. 'That's what you were looking for, isn't it?'

'Well, were there?' he demanded.

I shook my head. 'If there were, she must have deleted them.'

'How do I know I can believe you? Maybe you've kept them for . . . well, for whatever reason.'

'For blackmail? Is that what you're thinking? Though I can't imagine what anyone would have to blackmail you over.' I took her phone out of my purse. 'Check it out for yourself,' I said, handing it to him.

He took it and opened it to the shot of Doctor Welles. 'I wonder who he is,' he said, staring. 'Poor guy. I'll bet she had him by the goodies and wouldn't let go.'

'You don't want to know who he is,' I said. 'And I wouldn't tell you anyway. But the important thing is, that's the only one of that sort. Go ahead, see for yourself.'

He did, scrolling quickly through the

rest of the photos in the camera. 'Okay,' he said, 'you were telling me the truth.'

I remembered from a case my attorneys had tried that you could not really delete things from a computer. The files disappeared as ordered, but a real technician could still access them. I had a notion that probably this was true of these phone cameras as well, that those photos were still inside the thing somewhere, and an expert could retrieve them.

But that was something beyond my limited knowledge and technical abilities. Apparently Sam's too. And I saw no reason to disillusion him. The best thing to do, the smart thing, would be to destroy the phone altogether.

I put my hand out. 'And I'd like the phone back, if you don't mind. I promised to return it.' That was not true either, but he had no way of knowing that. I was getting pretty good at this business of fibbing.

For a moment, I thought he was going to hang on to it, but then with a show of reluctance he handed the phone back to me. I dropped it back into my purse.

'Sorry if I didn't trust you,' he said, 'but after her, I don't have a lot of faith in females.'

'But she did take incriminating photos of you?' I asked. 'That's what you were expecting to find, yes?' He nodded grimly. 'Nudes?'

'And worse. And not just me, either. It was like, practically everybody,' he said. 'Half the guys in that bar were in that phone at one time. Maybe half the guys in town. She swore she deleted them, but nobody believed her.'

'Were you one of her . . . ' I hesitated. I could not bring myself to say 'one of her lovers.' Whatever this had all been about, I was pretty sure love had not figured into it. 'Whatever,' I finished lamely.

'Yeah, I was one of her 'whatevers',' he said. He gave me a bitter kind of smile. 'You want to hear something really sad?' he asked. 'The truth was, I kind of liked the kid. Really.'

'I guessed that. The funeral. The flowers.' I shrugged.

'Yes. That was stupid of me, I guess.'

'Not really. Not if you liked her. I think

it was kind of sweet, to tell you the truth.'

He made a face. 'Look, the chick was messed up, big time, but I always thought somewhere inside, if you could ever get past all the crap, there was a good kid in there who'd just gone rotten somewhere, somehow.'

'I think you may have been right.'

'But you may as well know, it didn't do me any good, either, thinking that way. I tried to treat her right. I tried to talk to her about, you know, about stuff. About what she was doing to herself. But she didn't want to hear it. I was just another guy to her. One of many. What's the expression? E pluribus unum?'

'Latin. I think it's on the dollar bill,' I said with a smile.

'Is it?' he asked, and then, smiling back, 'Only with her, it wasn't about money. That wasn't the impression I was trying to give, if you think it was.'

'I didn't,' I said. 'I knew that.'

He looked me up and down. For the first time his smile looked genuine. 'You know, you're quite a girl,' he said.

'You think? Better than those chicks

you were with inside?'

We were standing just outside the door to the bar. Suddenly the door opened and the three women he had been with inside came out. They looked even scarier in the daylight.

'Speak of the devil,' I said in a whisper.

'Uh oh. Trouble,' he agreed.

'Hey, Marlowe,' one of them said in a loud voice. 'Who's your little friend?'

'Yeah,' another said, 'aren't you going to introduce us?'

He looked worried. 'The young lady was just . . . ' he started to say, and drew a blank. 'She was just about to . . . '

He was saved at that moment by the bell. Or, to be more precise, by the honk. A car horn blared behind me, and I looked over my shoulder to see Sarah pulling into the parking lot once more. She came to an abrupt stop just a few feet behind me and lowered the window on the passenger side.

'Beth,' she yelled out the open window, 'I was passing and I thought that was you. Need a lift?'

'The young lady was just about to

leave,' I said over his shoulder, finishing his remark for him. I ran to the waiting car and jumped in. The three women started to walk toward us. One of them was holding a beer bottle by its neck, like it was a club.

'Go,' I told Sarah under my breath, and she went, burning rubber. I put one hand out the window and waved bye to the group behind us before I put the window up and thought to lock the door.

'I felt bad leaving you there the way I did,' Sarah said when we were on the highway again. 'I hope I didn't mess anything up coming back for you.'

'I was never so glad to see anyone in my life,' I told her, and then we were both laughing the way we had used to do when we had gotten away with some really outrageous stunt back at Miss Parker's.

16

She dropped me this time back at the Lodge. Before I went inside, and after Sarah had driven away, I walked down to the water's edge with the phone in my hand, and tossed it as hard as I could into the water. I did not know a lot about phones and their cameras, but I felt pretty sure that a watery bath would take care of any remaining pictures. Just in case. Mrs. Rainey obviously knew nothing about the phone, so it was no loss to her. And I thought it better if no one else had access.

It had been a long and eventful day, and I was grateful to be back in my room; but as it turned out, this day was not finished with me yet.

I had cleaned myself up and repaired my makeup, and I was just preparing to go down to the dining room for dinner (chicken pot pie, so Mrs. Gershon had informed me as I came in) an hour or so later when my phone rang. I answered it to find a frantic-sounding Sarah on the other end of the line.

'The sheriff just called me,' she said. 'They've arrested Mike again, for assaulting Doctor Welles. I don't think I can deal with this alone. Please, can you go to the station with me?'

★   ★   ★

It turned out, in fact, that Mike had not been actually arrested. It was true that he had assaulted the doctor, but the sheriff was only holding him till we got there to pick him up.

'But it's only thanks to the kindness of Doctor Welles that he isn't under arrest,' the sheriff was quick to point out to us when we got there. 'The doctor refuses to press charges, even though I'd say your boy did a pretty good job of working him over. If you ask me, that's pretty gracious of the doc, not to say generous. I think you all owe him a big thank-you.'

'Yes, I have to say I agree,' I said. 'Very gracious.'

Of course, the sheriff did not know, as I

surely did, what the doctor was going to expect in return for his 'kindness.' It was a devil's bargain, but what could I do? If I reported him now for his malfeasance, Mike was sure to go to jail. Even in that other matter, Laurie's death, his arrest for assaulting her therapist was not likely to sit well with any jury. I had been effectively checkmated.

I admitted as much when I saw him the next day. 'I've decided not to make any kind of report on your sexual relationship with your client,' I said. 'Though I still think it was abhorrent.'

'I'm glad to hear it,' he said. At least he was gracious enough not to gloat, though we both knew he had won this particular round. 'I think this whole business has gone far enough.'

On the other hand, though, I will say, seeing the doctor, I thought Mike had done an adequate job of meting out justice. Welles had not one but two black eyes, and ugly bruises on his cheeks and chin, not to mention a split lip; and from the way he winced when he sat down or got up, I felt pretty sure his clothing was concealing plenty more bruises as well. So it was not as if his impropriety had gone unpunished. Of course, not losing his license meant that there was really nothing to stop him from doing the same thing in the future. But I hoped he'd learned a valuable lesson from this experience.

★ ★ ★

I had breakfast the following morning with Sarah, once again at that downtown diner with the perfect eggs and the shattering bacon. She seemed to me to be preoccupied, and over after-breakfast coffee, I asked her if there was anything bothering her.

'Oh. It's just . . . ' She hesitated. 'I had a conversation yesterday with Mother's doctor, Doctor Webster. And it was a little depressing.'

'Really? I thought you always told me that your mother was a hypochondriac.'

'I know, I used to think that. Oh, I knew her heart wasn't good. The doctor would hardly have had her on digitalis otherwise. But she's lost a lot of weight, and I could see lately that she was looking weakish. Yesterday I realized she was having trouble getting out of her chair. That's why I decided to call the doctor. I wanted to hear things directly from him, and not filtered through Anabelle. Which is usually what I get.'

'And?'

'A lot of the weakness is related to the heart problem, of course. As the doctor put it, when the pistons aren't firing right, the car loses power.'

I laughed despite myself. 'Is there anything besides the heart? Not that it isn't serious enough, but well, you know what I mean.'

'Unfortunately, there is. She seems,' she said, slowly stirring some sugar into her coffee, 'to be developing dementia.'

'Your mother? But she's always been so bright.'

'I think maybe they're the ones most at risk. Anyway, she's been forgetting things lately.'

'But we all do that, don't we? I know I do.'

'When I talked to her yesterday, she couldn't remember the name of the street where we used to live.'

'Apple Harvest Drive.'

'But she always knew that before. Now, all of a sudden, it seems to have gone right out of her mind. That kind of thing. I swear, a day or so ago she looked at me like she wasn't even sure who I was. She didn't say that, but I was sure that was what I saw in her eyes. She looked, oh, I don't know, confused, I guess is what I want to say.'

'You may be right.' I nodded. 'It happens, of course. I'm sorry. And to be frank, I thought when I saw her that she didn't look very healthy.'

'Mostly she's okay, I think. Her memory seems to come and go. The doctor still says if she sticks to her meds, she'll live to be one hundred. The only problem is, as he explained it, she may not know who I am by that time.' There was a definite catch in her voice as she said this.

'There isn't much anyone can do about these things, unfortunately.'

'I know. And for all her grumbling, Anabelle really does take good care of her. Better than I could. It's not that I don't want to, but the truth is, I'm just not the nurturing type. I never have been. Sick people depress me, and they sense it, so I bring them down too instead of perking them up.'

I had to laugh at that. 'I'm sorry,' I apologized for laughing, 'but it's hard to imagine Anabelle perking anybody up.'

She laughed too, but then quickly grew sober. 'I know what you mean. But she's conscientious, and I'd be more of a hindrance than a help, I think. I've decided to spend more time with Mother, anyway, and I've made up my mind to put my savings on the line and hire an attorney for Mike. Up to now, we've been thinking public defender, but I want someone on his side who has a vested interest in getting things cleared up.'

'Yes, I think he'd be far better off with his own hired and paid for attorney. Do you want me to talk to my people?'

She thought about that for a moment. 'They're kind of far away, aren't they?

Though if they know anybody local, anyone they could recommend, that would be a blessing.'

'I'll ask,' I promised. 'They might. I've learned working there that the world of lawyering is a small world.'

'Anyway, I think all that business with Mike has just added to Mom's stress. I think she'll be far more at ease knowing that's being handled as well as it can be.'

'What about hiring someone to look after her? A professional, I mean.'

'A nurse? Anabelle would have a fit if I hired a nurse.'

'But she complains about doing everything herself, doesn't she?'

'Yes, but that's just Anabelle. I've tried to help, believe me, lots of times. She just pushes me aside. She's a control freak. Mostly that drives other people crazy. Heck, it drives me crazy, to tell you the truth. But it works just fine when you're caring for someone. Everything is regimented and compartmentalized. There's not the slightest chance Mom would ever miss taking a pill. Not with Anabelle in charge.'

I personally thought she was being a bit sanguine about her sister. I agreed that Anabelle liked being in control, but woe betide the poor soul who ever got in her way. But this was their family, and their problem, and I was just an outsider. An outsider who, if she was smart, would keep her mouth shut. Some things were better left to be settled within the family.

17

Over the next week or so I made a point of visiting Mrs. Gladstone often, pretty much every day, sometimes with Sarah, sometimes not. I saw that Sarah was right: her mother was on the decline. A surprisingly swift decline, it seemed to me, though I knew it sometimes happened like that. She was losing weight, and looked a bit feebler each time that I saw her. And she was definitely more easily addled.

It was on one of those occasions when Sarah was not with me that I found myself, to my great surprise, having a cup of tea with Anabelle. On this occasion, Mrs. Gladstone had announced midway through my visit that she was tired. 'I feel like a nap,' she said.

'Then you should take one,' I said. I didn't add that I thought she looked tired.

'I agree,' Anabelle said. 'Come on,

Mother. I'll put you to bed.'

'Can I help?' I asked.

'You can talk to her while I get her out of those clothes and into a nightgown,' Anabelle said, and Mrs. Gladstone looked pleased by that suggestion.

'Oh, yes, please come with me,' she said. 'It'll be nice to have a talk while I get settled. Sarah tells me that she's looking for a legal firm to represent Mike.'

'Yes, I think that'll be best. Of course, it'd be even better if we could find out who killed that poor girl.'

'Why do you even care?' Anabelle asked.

'Because nobody else does,' I said. 'If we got Mike off, that would simply mean whoever really killed her would get off scot-free. That's not right, it seems to me.'

'Life doesn't always work out right,' Anabelle said.

'Which doesn't mean we shouldn't try to make it happen,' I argued. 'Besides, I can't help feeling sorry for that poor girl.'

Anabelle scoffed, but she left it at that.

'There you are, Mother. All ready for a nap.'

By this time, Mrs. Gladstone was in bed, the covers tucked up under her chin. I could see that she was ready to fall asleep. 'I'll just go now, and let you rest,' I said.

'Thank you,' she said, and just like that, her eyelids had dropped shut and her breathing had taken on that sleep-rhythm it assumed as one drifted off.

'I'm sorry your visit got cut short,' Anabelle said when we were back in the kitchen. 'She's like that a lot now, unfortunately. She gets tired so fast.'

'Yes. Sarah mentioned that too. But it's still sad to see. She was always such a vibrant person.'

'You get used to it. Especially when you see it every day.'

'It must be very difficult for you.'

Anabelle only shrugged. 'I think I'll make myself some tea. Would you like a cup?'

'Yes, I would,' I said, surprised. I can't say that Anabelle and I had ever been really antagonistic with one another, but I had never felt any real friendliness from her, either. So it was a bit unusual for her to invite me to stay and visit with her.

I won't pretend that it was exactly a love fest. The truth is, it was such an unusual occurrence that I think we were both a little uncomfortable with it. The conversation, what there was of it, was desultory. I was, in fact, about ready to go, having finished my tea, when Anabelle looked across the kitchen table and said, 'We're two of a kind, aren't we?'

'Are we?' I can't say I much liked the comparison. 'Why do you say that?'

'We're like those ghosts, both of us, it seems to me. The ones they say haunt the lake. Or maybe more like the ones Dickens wrote about. You're like, oh, I don't know, like the Ghost of Christmas Yet to Come, I suppose. I don't think you've really yet become what you could be, is what I mean. You seem to me to be mostly potential.'

'I'll have to think about that. And you? What ghost are you?'

She laughed. It was a surprisingly literary conversation to be having with

Anabelle. It was the first time, and perhaps the only time, that I had really taken any pleasure in sharing her company.

'Me?' she said. 'I'm the Ghost of Christmas Past. Definitely. I am what used to be, but is not anymore.' She thought about that for a moment. 'No, not anymore,' she said again. 'Everything's different now.'

She'd seemed to be in a light-hearted mood a moment before, but she sounded so somber when she said this that it frightened me. 'In what way?' I asked, but the old Anabelle was back as abruptly as she had taken her leave. It was like a curtain closed down over her face.

She shrugged and said, 'Oh, never mind. I was just making conversation. I didn't really mean anything by it. It's just a lot of nonsense anyway, if you ask me.'

There was more to those words she had spoken, however, than I realized at the time. If only I had paid more attention to what she was telling me. Or perhaps to what she was not telling me. So much sadness might have been averted had I only listened more carefully. But things are always simpler in hindsight, aren't they?

★   ★   ★

The next time I saw Anabelle, she was as cold as she had been friendly and warm on my last visit.

'You know,' she said when she saw me at their door, 'I can't have you upsetting Mother this way.'

'I didn't think I was. In fact,' I said, a bit annoyed at her implication, 'she seems to enjoy my visits. I think I might just be doing her some good.'

'Maybe,' she conceded grudgingly. 'Except she's always all worked up after you've been here. And that isn't good for her heart.'

'Maybe what's not good for her heart is being treated like a child,' I snapped, and was immediately sorry I had said it.

'I treat her like a child, as you put it, because she behaves like a child,' Anabelle replied angrily. 'And if you want the job of looking after her, I'd be happy to turn it over to you.'

'Anabelle, I'm sorry,' I said, feeling deflated. 'I shouldn't have said that. I'm sorry.'

'It's not easy, you know,' she went on, still too angry to accept my apology. 'You have no idea how difficult the woman can be.'

'I think I do,' I said abjectly. 'And I think you've been wonderful, the way you've taken care of her. And Sarah thinks the same.'

'Thank you,' she said, her anger burning off. 'But honestly, sometimes I think . . . ' But whatever she had been about to say, she apparently thought better of it. 'Oh, never mind,' she said instead, and added, 'Just try not to get her excited, please.'

'I promise.'

'And help me keep that silly dog out of her room.'

'Daisy? But what harm can she do?'

Anabelle did not deign to answer, but only gave me one of her fierce scowls.

As it happened, on my next visit I saw Anabelle, but not Mrs. Gladstone.

This time was nothing more than a spur of the moment visit. I had gone to the stationery shop downtown to pick up some greeting cards I wanted, and since I was only a couple of blocks away, I decided I would stop by and say hello.

I was just mounting the steps to the back door when I heard Anabelle say behind me, 'Don't bother knocking. She's sound asleep.'

'Is she?' I asked, turning. Anabelle was just coming along, down by the water's edge, walking Daisy.

'She was when I left a few minutes ago.' She had Daisy on a leash and was carrying her 'friend,' that baseball bat. She bent down to unclip Daisy's leash from her collar. The poodle ran up to greet me and, after hopping up and down and wagging her tail to show her pleasure at seeing me, she ran on by and stopped on the top step, alternately staring at the door and looking back to be certain

Anabelle got the message.

'I just went out to walk the dog, but she was asleep when I left her,' Anabelle said. 'Oh, excuse me. Something I've got to do. We've got visitors, looks like.'

She plucked a couple of good-sized rocks off the ground, and tossing one of them into the air, batted it as if it were a baseball. The rock landed near some bushes along the path. Anabelle threw the second rock and batted it as well. This one went directly into the bushes, and elicited a startled yelp. I had a quick glimpse of something brown and low darting out of the bush and running swiftly away.

'Coyotes,' Anabelle said. 'They see Daisy and start thinking of something to eat. Of course, they don't come too close to the house anymore. You just saw why they stay clear. But if I pay them no mind for a while, they start getting bolder. Next thing you know, they'll be having Daisy home for dinner.'

'You're pretty good with that thing,' I said, indicating the bat in her hands.

'Practice,' was all she said. She went

past me and opened the door to let Daisy into the house. 'I'll tell Mother you were here. When she wakes up.' She followed Daisy inside and closed the door firmly.

I guess I've gotten the message, I thought. But as I started to walk away, I thought I heard Mrs. Gladstone inside welcoming Daisy home.

I kept going. Of course, I told myself, the fact that Mrs. Gladstone was awake now, if she truly was (and I was not altogether sure of what I had or had not heard), it did not mean that she had not been asleep when Anabelle left her a few minutes earlier.

I was trying to give Anabelle the benefit of every doubt. Because the only alternative I could think of was that, for some reason or other, she was trying to keep me away from her mother. Which surely made no sense. How could I be any kind of threat?

* * *

It was the same evening, after that odd conversation, when I got a text message on my phone from Mrs. Gladstone, once again telling me she had something she wanted to share with me. I was back at the Lodge at that time, and without a car, but it was only a short stroll to their cottage, and without phoning Sarah for a lift, I decided again that I would walk there.

Anabelle did not look pleased to see me at their door. 'Your mother sent me a text message,' I said. 'That's why I'm here.'

'Did she, now?' Anabelle looked surprised. 'What did it say?'

'Apparently there was something she wanted to tell me, but she didn't say what it was. I suppose she wanted to tell me in person.'

'Yes, that sounds like her, all right.' Anabelle looked me over as if I might be trying to play some kind of trick on her. 'Well, come in, and let's ask her what it was, why don't we? But I have to warn you, before you see her, she's gotten mighty forgetful. Sometimes even confused about things. Don't be surprised if she acts a bit addled.'

What did surprise me when I saw her

was that Mrs. Gladstone was now in a wheelchair, Daisy perched on her lap.

'Isn't it nice?' Mrs. Gladstone asked when I stared at the contraption in which she sat. 'My legs were getting weak, so the doctor prescribed this for me. It's motorized, see.' She demonstrated its mobility for me, scooting back and forth briefly across the linoleum. The ride seemed to delight Daisy. Doggy Disneyland, I found myself thinking.

'The last time I fell,' Mrs. Gladstone went on, 'Anabelle had to carry me to bed. Now all she'd have to do is get me into my chair. In fact, as long as I'm in the chair, I'm not likely to fall, period.'

'That dog,' Anabelle started to say, reaching for the animal. 'She shouldn't be in here.'

'Leave her alone,' her mother said, holding up a hand. 'Daisy's keeping me company.'

'She's aggravating you, is what she's doing,' Anabelle said.

'If she is, it's a very pleasant kind of aggravation. She'll stay where she is, thank you. And if she needs to go out, you won't even have to be bothered; I can run this chair over to the back door and let her out myself. And back in, too.'

Anabelle took a step back, seeming to accept the dismissal. 'Beth says there was something you wanted to talk to her about,' she said.

'Was there?' Mrs. Gladstone looked from one of us to the other, seeming confused.

'She says you sent her a text message.'

'Did I? Oh, dear, I don't remember.'

'You don't remember sending her a message? Or you don't remember what you wanted to tell her?'

'I don't remember either one,' Mrs. Gladstone said with a little whimper.

I was watching her carefully when she said this, actually staring hard at her. I suddenly realized that Mrs. Gladstone was staring back at me, just as hard. For all her seeming confusion, I had the distinct impression that she was putting on an act. That she was not really as addled as she seemed to be. But why? I wondered. There were only the three of us there, four if you counted Daisy. And surely anything Mrs. Gladstone had to say could only be local gossip. Family gossip, more than likely, since she hardly went anywhere now, and certainly not since she had acquired that chair. But what could she possibly want to say of that nature that she did not want Anabelle to hear? Because, though I might have been mistaken, that was certainly the impression I got.

'I think,' Anabelle said, 'maybe I'm going to have to take that phone away from you.'

'Oh, no, please don't.' Her phone was on Mrs. Gladstone's lap. She snatched it up now and clutched it protectively to her bosom.

'But apart from texting Beth, which now you don't even remember, when do you use it?'

'I want it in case I have to call somebody. A friend, maybe. Or Sarah.'

'If there's something you need to say to Sarah, you can just tell me,' Anabelle said. 'And I can relay the message to her.'

'It's not the same thing that way. What if I just wanted to hear Sarah's voice? Oh, please, Anabelle, I need the phone. I'd feel so lost without it.'

'Lost? In what way, lost?'

'I don't know. I'd just feel so disconnected from everything. And everyone.'

'Maybe.' Anabelle continued to glower at her. 'But anyone can see how stressed out you are at the moment. Not to mention that you sent Beth a message, and now you don't remember doing that. I can't have you getting yourself all worked up like this. It's not good for your heart. And it's bad for my nerves, too, I can tell you that.'

'I won't cause you any more aggravation. I won't, I promise.' Mrs. Gladstone gave a little laugh and waved one hand vaguely in the air, though I noticed that she continued to hold her phone close with the other hand. 'Daisy and I will be as quiet and as meek as little lambs, won't we, Daisy? And Beth, dear, I'm sorry if I have caused you any alarm for nothing. The next time — '

'The next time,' Anabelle finished for her, addressing me directly, 'just don't pay any attention when she sends you that kind of message. It doesn't mean anything, and it's just likely to get her all upset.'

'Of course,' I said. 'I didn't mean to cause any trouble.'

'It's not you, it's her. And that damned phone.'

I stayed for a bit longer, and we engaged in some chit-chat, Mrs. Gladstone and I, with Anabelle keeping a close eye on us and her ears cocked. Daisy turned around in a circle a couple of times, settled her snout on her paws, and went to sleep.

I left within the half hour, but as I walked the now-dark streets back to the Lodge, I could not shake the feeling that I had just missed something, something significant.

But what it had been, I had no clue.

18

I did not hear from Mrs. Gladstone over the next few days, although whenever I saw Sarah she updated me on her mother's progress. Or, as fate would have it, lack thereof.

'Every day, when I see her, I can tell that she's gone a little further downhill, and she's picking up speed as she goes,' Sarah said. 'Plus, these days she seems to be spending more and more of her time in bed. That's surely not a good sign.'

'I think you're right about that,' I said, but my thoughts were elsewhere. I was thinking of that strange impression I had gotten on my last visit, that there was something Mrs. Gladstone wanted to say to me that she did not want her daughter to hear. But surely I must have been mistaken in that. Wasn't I? With dementia, it was difficult to know exactly what you were seeing. Or hearing.

I had dinner that evening downstairs in the Lodge's dining room, a delicious rib roast this time with a Yorkshire pudding that would have done even the pickiest Anglophile proud. I had left my phone in my room, and when I returned it was to discover that again I had a message, telling me that I had missed a call from Mrs. Gladstone. How puzzling, I thought, remembering the last time this happened. Would she even remember why she contacted me?

I started to call her back, and remembered the odd impression I had gotten that on that occasion that she did not want to talk to me in front of her daughter. I might have been mistaken, of course, but I decided instead that I would walk the few blocks to their cottage and try to talk to her in person.

In any case, although there had been no pie tonight, there had been a delicious chocolate cake instead, obviously hand-made rather than store bought (the crumb is always the giveaway); and I had, rather shamelessly I admit, asked for a second slice. So a good brisk walk would no doubt do wonders for my waistline.

When I looked out my window, I saw that it had started to rain, although not terribly hard. I still had that poncho of Sarah's, and I donned it before starting out. The town had few streetlights, and the street where the Gladstones lived, like most of the town's streets, had no sidewalks, so I was walking more or less in the street. I had gone not much more than a block down it when I heard a car behind me. I thought at once of Deputy Willis. Surely he was not still keeping an eye on me?

I stopped right in the roadway, in the way of any car approaching from behind, and waited for him to steer around me, fully prepared to give him a piece of my mind. But the car turned a corner before it got to where I was standing. I heard the sound of its motor fading into the distance.

Now you're being paranoid, I told myself. Feeling a bit foolish, I continued on my way. A dog barked nearby, declaring that I was perhaps too close to his turf, but he did nothing more than make noise, so I ignored his complaints and walked on.

It was night by the time I got there. I could see the kitchen lights were aglow in the house as I approached, and the living room dark, so I went around to the back and knocked at the door. Anabelle must have been close at hand because she answered almost at once. When she saw me, she gave me a decidedly frosty look. So much for our developing friendship, I thought.

'What do you want?' she demanded in a stern voice. She stood smack dab in the doorway, blocking it with her large frame, and making me feel like an intruder.

'I came to see your mother,' I told her, thinking, *So much for hospitality*. If I told her that her mother had phoned me again, I would probably never get inside the house, or I would cost her mother the phone. It seemed to me that Anabelle was only looking for an excuse to take it away permanently. I did not want to become that excuse.

'She's asleep,' she said, but at almost the very same moment a voice from inside called out, 'Anabelle, is that Beth Nolan? Is she there? I thought I heard her voice.'

'I guess she woke up,' I said, smiling sweetly.

Anabelle gave a grunt of displeasure, but she did step aside to let me come in. 'I'll see if she's up to company,' she said, adding in the way of explanation, 'She's been feeling sick lately. I don't want her to be bothered.'

'Never mind,' I said, ignoring her offer. 'I'm not going to bother her, and I know the way.' I swept by her and into the kitchen, but I paused there. That little white bundle lying in the corner, surely that wasn't Daisy, I thought. She did not appear to be moving at all, and even at a distance I could see a red stain on the floor beneath her.

Anabelle saw me staring. 'Daisy's had an accident,' she said.

'Oh, goodness,' I said, and started toward the bundle, but Anabelle stepped into my path, blocking my way. 'I'll take care of it,' she said. 'Go, make your visit.'

'But, I can see . . . ' I started to argue.

'Beth?' Mrs. Gladstone cried from the bedroom. 'Are you there?'

'You'd better go on in if you want to see her,' Anabelle said. 'She'll be asleep soon. I'm surprised she's not already. I'll see to the dog.' Her tone of voice brooked no argument.

Mrs. Gladstone was at least in bed when I came into her room, which I suppose might have accounted for Anabelle's insistence that she was already asleep, though she was clearly wide awake now. Or she might even have been asleep earlier. I wanted to give Anabelle every excuse for her rudeness. And, of course, even if Anabelle had been untruthful, I could not altogether fault her for it. She did have the responsibility of caring for her mother, and she had already expressed her concern about things that disturbed her. Such as, I thought with some embarrassment, an unexpected visitor.

I tried to tell myself that it was not blood I saw on the baseball bat leaning against the wall by the refrigerator as I went by it. Something crimson. But surely not blood. Only, I could not just at the moment think of anything so red.

'Beth,' Mrs. Gladstone greeted me from her bed with a bright smile. 'How wonderful to see you. What brings you by?' She looked as if she welcomed my visit and was not at all disturbed by it, which relieved my chagrin to no little degree.

'I had a message that you had called me earlier,' I told her. 'I thought there might be some kind of emergency, so I came as soon as I got it.'

'Oh, how sweet of you to worry about me,' she gushed. 'But, no, it wasn't anything like that. It's just that I've been in bed for the last three days. My heart, you know. And to be honest, I was just feeling lonesome and bored. You know how that is, I'm sure. Sarah's gone over to Mike's trailer for the evening. It seems he was feeling a bit down, so she said she'd keep him company. And that left me all alone.'

'Anabelle's here,' I said.

She gave me a mischievous smile. 'Anabelle's not the chatty type,' she said in a lowered voice. 'And that's what I wanted, someone to chat with for a while.'

'Well, I'm here now,' I said, a bit disappointed to discover that I might have over reacted to the summons. I pulled a chair over next to her bed and seated myself in it. 'And we can chat all you want. I can stay as long as you like, too, but promise to let me know when you start feeling tired, and I promise in turn that I'll get out of your hair.' *And out of Anabelle's*, I started to say, and thought better of that.

'That's nice, and I promise that if I start feeling tired or sleepy, I'll let you know. But right now I'm fine.'

'Okay, then, where should we start? I'm all ears. Chat away.'

She beamed, but she seemed in no real hurry for conversation. She sighed and leaned back against the pillows. 'Isn't this pleasant. I've been wanting some company. You just can't imagine how lonely I get some days. Oh, have you seen little

Daisy, by the way? I called her and called her, but she didn't come. I hope she hasn't gotten herself into trouble. I have no idea what gets into her.'

'Daisy? Oh, I . . . ' I floundered, not sure what I should or should not say.

'Daisy's had an accident,' Anabelle said, coming into the bedroom behind me.

'An accident? What kind of accident?' Mrs. Gladstone leaned forward in her bed, alarmed.

'Frankly, a rather bizarre one,' Anabelle said.

'Oh?'

'Yes. I . . . ' Anabelle paused, as if thinking how to express herself. 'Well, I'd just waxed the kitchen floor. You know how slick it can be when I wax it. Until it dries, it's like walking on ice.'

'Yes,' Mrs. Gladstone said. 'Don't tell me she fell.'

'No, she didn't fall exactly. She slid.'

Mrs. Gladstone laughed. 'That must have been a sight. Daisy, ice-skating.'

'It was funny, yes. But the thing is, I had that bottom cabinet drawer pulled all the way out, you know, the one I was intending to clean. I told you about that.'

'Did you?' Mrs. Gladstone looked confused. 'I don't remember.'

'Yes, I did tell you,' Anabelle said sharply. 'You've just forgotten, is all. But I did tell you that was what I was going to do this evening.'

'I suppose I did forget,' Mrs. Gladstone said with a sigh. 'I'm sorry. I'm such a nuisance, I know.'

'It's not important,' Anabelle said, sounding not at all gracious.

'But it is,' Mrs. Gladstone said. 'It is to me, at least. I hate not being able to remember things.'

Anabelle looked at her for a moment as if she did not know what to say. Finally, she just went on with her explanation: 'Anyway, Daisy slid on the wet wax. As I said before, it was like ice, it was so slippery, and she slid right into that open drawer that was sticking out. The bottom one. Cracked her head on it, in fact.'

'Oh dear, I hope she isn't hurt. Beth, did you see her? Is she okay?'

'I think she's . . . ' I started to say, and

could not get the words out.

'She's dead,' Anabelle said brusquely.

'Oh.' Mrs. Gladstone gave a wail of pain. 'Oh, not my little Daisy. But, how could she . . . on an open drawer, you said?'

'She hit it hard,' Anabelle said.

'I must go to her,' Mrs. Gladstone said, struggling to get out of bed.

'No,' Anabelle said firmly. 'You stay where you are. I'll take care of her.'

'Oh, dear.' Mrs. Gladstone sank back on her pillows. 'If you insist,' she said meekly.

'I do. You lie there and chat with Beth.' With that, Anabelle left the room.

As abruptly as that, Mrs. Gladstone seemed to have forgotten Daisy altogether. She glanced at the door, to be sure Anabelle really had gone. Then she gave me a sly smile. 'Look what I have,' she said, holding up her phone.

'Yes, I knew you had it. You must have, since you called me on it.'

'Oh, yes, I hadn't thought of that.'

'So what makes your phone so important?'

'Don't you remember? I'm not supposed to have it. Anabelle took it away.'

'Did she? I know she threatened to, but I didn't know she actually had.'

'She did. It couldn't have been more than an hour ago. She came right up to the bed and stuck out her hand, and said I had to give it to her.'

'Then how do you happen to have it now?' I could not imagine Anabelle changing her mind once she had made it up to something.

'I'm not supposed to. She meant to take it with her when she left the room, but she was busy with some other stuff. Now let me think, what was she doing? Oh, I remember. She wanted to put some lotion on my hands; they've gotten so dry lately. And she laid the phone on the dresser, just over there. But she must've forgotten about it.'

'So you see,' I said, 'It's not just you. Everyone forgets things.'

'That's true, but not the way I do.'

'Maybe you're just being hard on yourself.'

'No, no, it's terrible the way I forget

everything. Anabelle yells at me for it all the time.'

'She shouldn't do that.'

'That's nice of you to say, but I think she's right. Now, where was I? I was telling you something . . . '

'The phone,' I prompted her.

'Oh, yes, the phone, that's what it was.' I nodded. 'Well, she left it on top of the dresser and forgot it was there. So when she went out and left it, and I saw it there, I got out of bed — oh, that's scary for me these days; I always think I'm going to fall, and it would've been really bad just then, as you can imagine. Anabelle would've come in to help me back up, and I'd have caught hell for being out of bed in the first place, not to mention for having the phone after she took it away from me.

'But I was very, very careful. I took hold of the edge of the dresser to keep myself from falling. You should have seen how clever I was, and how careful. And as soon as I had the phone, I crept right back into bed. I did sort of fall then, but I fell across the bed, so it was all right, I just had to scramble around a bit. And once I was lying back down, with the covers over me and everything, I think that's when I called you, while I still had the phone. But, you know, if she remembers where she left it, which she's bound to do sooner or later, she'll come looking for it, and she'll take it away from me again. Only this time she won't leave it lying where I can get hold of it so easily.'

'But why does she want to take it away from you?' I asked. 'Doesn't it give some company when you get lonesome? You can always call someone to chat with them. You can always call me. Or Sarah. That's a good thing, isn't it?'

'You'd think so, wouldn't you? That's how I feel too. But she says it just aggravates me. She meant to take it clear out of the room, I'm sure she did. But she forgot . . . Oh.' She looked about a bit distractedly.

'Is anything wrong?' I asked. 'You look like you're upset.'

'There was something I wanted to tell

you. That's why I called you in the first place.'

'And what was that?' Maybe at last we would get to the bottom of those mysterious calls.

But instead of explaining, she gave me a shamefaced look. 'It's embarrassing to have to tell you, but I've forgotten,' she said. 'I know it was something important, but for the life of me, I can't think what it was. Maybe Anabelle's right.'

'Don't worry about it,' I said, disappointed. 'It'll come back to you in its own time, I'm sure.'

'Oh, it's nothing, I guess,' she said. 'Nothing too important, anyway. In the meantime, though . . . Oh,' she exclaimed again, 'I've just thought of something.'

'Have you remembered what you wanted to tell me?'

'I just thought of my ring.'

'Your ring?' I couldn't imagine anything she might want to tell me about her ring.

'Yes. I need to ask you for a favor.'

'Of course. Ask away. I'll be happy to do anything I can.'

'It's just, well, it seems to have vanished.'

'Your ring's vanished?'

'For some reason, I can't find it. You know the ring I mean, the diamond with the emeralds.'

'I've seen it,' I said drily, but she did not notice my sarcasm.

'I swear, it was right here on the nightstand a new minutes ago. Did I already tell you, Anabelle wanted to rub some lotion on my hands earlier because they're so dry and chapped? Would you look at them?'

'They do look like they could use some help,' I said. She seemed to be rambling, but I had the feeling that sooner or later, in her own time, she would get to a point.

'They're terrible, I swear. They're like sandpaper. So, where was I? Oh, I remember. Yes, so that's when I took my ring off, and I'm sure I put it on the nightstand, right here by the bed, and that was when she laid the phone on the dresser too, and well, you know about that. But now my ring's up and disappeared. It's not on the nightstand.'

I looked, but the surface of the nightstand was clear. 'No, it's not there,' I agreed.

'Then it must have gotten knocked off somehow, is all I can think. Could you be a dear and look on the floor, Beth, just there by the bed, and see if you spot it? It might have gotten brushed off the nightstand accidentally while we were fiddling around with the hand lotion.'

'It shouldn't be difficult to see,' I said, and got obediently on my knees by the side of the bed.

She laughed. 'I wouldn't have thought so,' she said. 'The diamond's very big. I forget how many carats. Four, I think, or five. Anyway, I don't think I've ever seen a bigger one.'

'It's enormous,' I agreed. But I found no trace of the ring on the floor, despite pushing the bedcovers aside and looking under there, just in case it had rolled after falling.

'Hello,' Anabelle said from the door-way. 'Is this some new kind of game we're playing? Let's get down and crawl around on the floor? You'll have to excuse me, but

I don't think my knees would like that.'

I looked up. She had come in bearing a tray with a large steaming mug sitting atop it.

'Your mother seems to have lost her ring,' I said in the way of explanation, standing and brushing myself off.

'It was right there on the nightstand, Anabelle,' Mrs. Gladstone said. 'And now it's just gone and disappeared. I can't imagine what happened to it. It can't have been taken. There's been nobody in the house but us. And then Beth, of course, but she didn't take it.'

'We thought it might have fallen on the floor,' I said. 'I was looking to see if it was down there, but I saw no trace of it.'

'If you want my opinion, it's probably somewhere in the bed with her,' Anabelle said, sitting her tray on the nightstand. 'She's lost so much weight lately, and it doesn't want to stay on her finger. I've told her and told her that she's going to lose it for good if she isn't careful.'

'I *am* careful,' Mrs. Gladstone said in a petulant voice. 'You know I'm careful, Beth.'

'Never mind,' Anabelle said. 'You wait and see. It's in the bed, I'd swear to it. She'll find it when she rolls over on it and the diamond stabs her in the backside. I've brought your tea, Mother.'

'Oh good, it'll put me to sleep.'

Anabelle plumped up a pillow and put it against the headboard, and helped her mother to sit up.

'What's that?' Anabelle asked. She was looking at the phone, lying atop the bedspread beside her mother, but Mrs. Gladstone ignored the question. For all the interest she showed, you might have thought the phone was invisible.

'I would've sworn I put this away,' Anabelle said, snatching the phone up and dropping it into her pocket. She gave her mother a suspicious look.

'Why can't she have a phone?' I asked.

'Because . . . because . . . it's not good for her. It gets her too excited.'

'I don't see . . . ' I started to say.

'You don't see what I have to go through with her each and every day,' Anabelle snapped. Which I translated as, 'Mind your own business.' Which, I had to admit, she was entitled to say.

Mrs. Gladstone seemed not to hear this exchange, or if she did, she had decided to ignore it. She reached for the cup on the tray instead and took a sip of her tea.

'Umm, lovely,' she said. 'But it tastes different. It's not the chamomile, is it, dear?'

'It's a new flavor. I thought you might like it,' Anabelle said. 'And don't ask me what flavor, I've completely forgotten since I looked at the box. Drink up, now, Mother.'

Greta Gladstone did as she was told, taking another big sip from the cup before returning it to the tray. 'It's delicious,' she said. 'It has a floral taste. What did you say it was?'

'I didn't.' Anabelle waved a vague hand. 'And I really don't remember. Hibiscus, maybe?'

'No, not hibiscus, I don't think,' Mrs. Gladstone said, tilting her head thoughtfully to one side. 'Though I love hibiscus tea. But it's familiar. I'll think of it in a minute.'

'You do that. In the meantime, I'll just take the tray back to the kitchen.' Anabelle set the cup aside and took the tray with her out of the room.

Mrs. Gladstone and I were left alone. 'Do you want to lie down?' I asked her. 'I can move that pillow if you want.'

'In a minute. I think I'll have a bit more of my tea, though. It really is delicious.' She reached for the cup on the nightstand and took another large gulp from it, frowning as she swallowed. 'It is odd, I feel like I ought to recognize this but I don't. It's so familiar. But I still wonder what happened to my ring. You're sure it's not down there on the floor somewhere?'

'Certain,' I said. 'I looked carefully.'

She had another drink of her tea. Her face suddenly lit up. 'You know, I'd almost swear this is . . . ' She stopped before she said it. 'But I must be wrong, it couldn't be. Anabelle knows better. She'd never make a mistake like that. She's too careful about . . . '

But she did not finish what she had been going to say. The cup slipped from her hand, clattering to the floor and spilling its contents on bedclothes and carpet. As suddenly as that, she had begun to retch violently, staining her nightgown and the bedclothes, and to shake all over, so violently that the headboard clattered noisily against the wall.

19

'Mrs. Gladstone — Greta!' I cried, trying to no avail to hold her still. 'Anabelle, come here — something's wrong!' I shouted.

'What is it?' Anabelle rushed in from the room next door.

'Your mother, she's having some kind of fit,' I said. 'Call nine one one, hurry, and tell them to . . . ' But the words caught in my throat when I turned to look at her. Anabelle was wearing *the ring*.

She saw me staring at it, and waved her hand as if it were of no consequence. 'Oh, this. It was in the kitchen,' she said, 'lying on the counter. She must've left it there.' She turned to run from the room.

'Where are you going?' I shouted after her.

'To call nine one one,' she called back. 'Stay with her.'

'Beth,' Mrs. Gladstone managed to say

in a tremulous whisper, 'the tea, it's . . . '
But she could say no more. Her eyes
rolled back in her head. She gave a great
moan that turned into an ominous rattle
in her throat, and slumped over on the
pillows. I felt carefully for a pulse. There
wasn't one.

She was dead.

What had she been trying to tell me
about the tea? Whatever it had been, it
was important enough for a dying woman
to try to explain to me.

I got down on my knees again, on the
floor, and found the cup where it had
fallen by the side of the bed. There were
no more than some dregs of the tea left, a
small puddle of liquid in the bottom of
the cup. I held the cup to my nose and
sniffed at it.

The scent was unmistakable: oleander.
Poisonous, but not generally fatal to
humans, unless in combination with
digitalis. In which case it was deadly
indeed. But how could that have happened? As her mother had tried to say,
Anabelle certainly knew better.

I heard footsteps approaching, and

without looking up, I started to say, 'Anabelle, this tea seems to be . . . '

I did look up then, to find myself staring at the barrel of a shotgun. Anabelle was holding it in the crook of one arm, and it was aimed directly at me.

'It's oleander,' I finished lamely. 'The tea. Isn't it?'

'Is it? How strange. I wonder how that could've happened.' Anabelle smiled and batted her eyelashes in mock innocence.

'I wonder too.'

'Maybe she made it herself,' she said. 'We all heard her that day, the day you arrived, talking about making some tea from the plants. If she's asked, my sister can attest to that.'

'But your mother told me she hadn't been out of bed in three days,' I said. She laughed.

'Well, she lied, I suppose. She must've been out of bed to find her phone.'

'But the phone was on the dresser, right there.' I pointed. 'At least that's what she told me.'

'She might've lied about that too. Oh, gosh, let's be charitable and say she got confused, which has been happening a lot lately. Or, since she was out of bed already, maybe she went into the kitchen and made herself some tea while she was there.'

'I *know* she hadn't been out of her bed since I got here. And you brought her the tea yourself. You said you'd brewed it for her, when you brought it in on the tray.'

'What tray is that?' she asked.

Of course, there was no tray in the room. 'You took it back to the kitchen,' I said. 'I saw you. I could swear to that.'

'Yes, Anabelle said. 'I suppose you could swear to that. If you were asked.'

'But I'm not going to be asked, is that what you're implying?'

'In any case, it can hardly matter one way or another,' she said with a tone of finality. 'She'll be out of that bed soon. Out of it forever. She's dead, isn't she?'

'Yes. And there's no point in pretending how it happened. You killed her. How could you, Anabelle? You murdered your own mother! For, what, a diamond ring?' I gestured at the ring on her finger, glinting wickedly in the pale light.

'It wasn't for the ring,' Anabelle said loudly and angrily. 'She was an endless nag. You only saw her on her best behavior, but she could be a bitch. And lately she'd turned into a *helpless* bitch. Yes, she *had* been in that bed for three days. But it felt to me more like it was three years. I had to spoon feed her everything, just like a helpless infant. Bathe her, dress her. And, yes, I had to change her diapers, too. Do you have any idea what a disgusting chore that is, changing someone's diapers? An adult's diapers?'

'You're not the only child who's ever had to care for an aging parent,' I said.

She snorted her scorn. 'Maybe not. But I'm the only one in this household, I can tell you that. You heard Sarah. She couldn't do it because she couldn't remember things. Like her mother. Or, she had a million other excuses. Everything was left up to me. Everything. I just plain got tired of doing it all.'

'I'm sure Mike would've helped, if you'd only asked him.'

'Mike?' She laughed bitterly. 'He was

too busy drooling over that little trollop of his. That worthless young slut who moved in with him.'

A light went on then over my head. 'It was you,' I said. Suddenly it was all clear to me.

'What do you mean?' She narrowed her eyes.

'You killed her, Laurie Rainey. It was you, wasn't it?'

At first, I thought she was going to deny it. A part of me still hoped that she would, that I was mistaken and that she could honestly deny it. But she could not. And, in my heart, I already knew it was true.

'Yes,' she said after a long moment, fairly spitting the word at me. 'I killed her. And you want to know what else? I would've done it a long time ago if I'd only gotten the chance. She deserved it. She deserved to die.'

'But why? What harm could she possibly have done you? Why kill that poor unhappy girl?'

'Why? I'll tell you why. Because I watched her all that time, month after month, year after year, draining the life out of him. You think she was unhappy? You didn't see my brother while she worked her wiles on him. You talk about unhappy. He was the unhappy one.'

'But he says she was a good person. He loved her. And I think she loved him, too. What did she do to him?'

'You only ask that because you weren't here to see it happening. She was turning him into another sex-crazed man, like all the others.'

'Mike? Your brother? I don't believe that.'

'It's true. He was becoming just like the ones who skulk around in the dark, looking for women to prey on. I see them every time I go out, watching me, always watching to see when I might drop my guard. And that was what she intended for him, what he was going to become, if no one freed him from her.'

'But Mike wasn't like that,' I cried. 'I don't believe it. I can't believe it.'

'She wasn't through with him yet. She was still working on him.'

'And I suppose you just happened to

stumble across them that night, in the park?'

'Yes, I did,' she said. 'I wasn't following them, if that's what you're implying. I was just out walking. I had to get away from that woman, my mother, you understand. I was ready to kill her then, to tell you the truth. There were so many days. It was all I could do. If you only knew what it was like.'

'And you found them instead.'

'I was down by the lake, at the park there, the one that runs along the shore, and I saw them. I saw what she tried on with him, the little tramp. She wanted him to . . . to . . . I can't even say it. But I knew. I saw it with my own eyes. You want to hear the truth? I'll tell you the truth. I was never as proud of my brother as I was that night when he walked away from her.'

'Then why kill her?'

'Because she wasn't through with him, I tell you. She would never have been finished with him, not until she'd destroyed him.'

'You can't know that.'

'Ha! But I do know, as it happens. I heard it from the horse's mouth, as they say.'

'What do you mean?'

'I heard it from the girl herself.'

'Laurie said that?' I asked, incredulous. 'I don't believe it.'

'It's true, whether you believe it or not. Oh, maybe she didn't say it exactly like that, not in so many words, no. And before you accuse me of making anything up, you may as well know I tried to talk to her. I went over to her that night, after he'd gone. She was still lying on the ground where he'd thrown her when she tried her disgusting tricks on him. But she was trying to get up, and she was still calling his name, begging him to come back to her. That was when I knew the truth. Not the way you try to fantasize things, to make everything sound like a fairy tale. There are no fairy tales. No fairy godmothers. No happy endings. I made the ending, the right one, to save my brother.'

'You broke his heart.'

'He'll get over it. Believe me, in time

he'll be glad he was saved. I did the right thing. I'm sure of it.'

'But you might not have needed to do anything. It all might've ended then, that night. They might never have been together again, after that quarrel. There may have been no reason for you to do what you did.'

'I did what had to be done. Regardless of your wishful thinking, it wasn't going to end there. I knew that, not unless I did something.'

'But how can you be so sure of that?'

'Because I asked her,' she said vehemently. 'I tried to talk to her. I even begged her just to leave him alone.'

'And she wouldn't?'

'Hah! Fat chance. She laughed at me. She called me a dried-up old prune. Told me to mind my own business. That's how remorseful she was. She called me names.'

'And you hit her,' I said. 'With that baseball bat you carry.'

'Yes, I did. Only, she was still laughing. Even after I had hit her. There was blood running down the side of her head, into her eyes, everywhere, and she was still laughing. At me. So then I hit her again. I had to, to make her stop laughing. And after that, I don't remember what happened. Everything gets blurry. I must've kept on hitting her, I think, because when they found her, they said her head was nothing but a pulp. They thought Mike must've beaten her to death with a rock.'

She looked dazed for a moment. I had been kneeling on the floor all this time. Now I got slowly to my feet, carefully, so as not to startle her. 'Anabelle,' I said, 'you're not well. Sarah was right. You've been under too much stress. I understand, believe me, I do. Caring for your mother, all that responsibility, everything was on your shoulders. No one can suffer all that pressure and not bend to it.'

'Some even break,' she said dully.

'That's true. And I can see what a burden it must've been. Let me take you away. There are people who can help you. I'll get you help, I promise.'

'No,' she said, suddenly shaking off her lethargy and brandishing that shotgun at me threateningly. 'We're not going anywhere. Well, you aren't, anyway. Anywhere, that is, except out on the lake.'

'The lake? But we can't go out on the lake. It's nighttime, and it's raining. It isn't safe.' Since I had come in, the rain had worsened. I could hear it beating against the window. One window was cracked slightly, and the curtain over it billowed inward like a beckoning hand. Beckoning me to what?

'Yes.' She glanced at the window. 'Yes, it's storming out there. So what? Are you afraid you might drown?' She laughed wickedly.

'It's not just me. We might both drown.'

'Me too, you mean? Not likely. I know that lake like I know the back of my hand,' she scoffed. 'But you're a different story. Suppose you took our boat, say without asking permission, and went out in it. At night. In a storm. Lots of people have heard you say you wanted to see our ghosts. That's when you would have to go out to look for them, at night, in a storm. That's what people believe. So, who's to say you didn't decide to take matters into your own hands and go out to try to find them?'

'I'm not going to take the boat out,' I said. 'Not tonight. Not ever!'

'Really? I think you're wrong.'

I knew then where this was leading. 'You want to kill me, the same as you killed your mother,' I said. 'Only, in my case, it'll be out on the lake.'

'There are plenty of bodies in that water already, plenty of them,' she said. 'One more won't make it overflow its banks.'

'I won't . . . ' I started to say, but my objections were overruled.

'March,' she ordered, waving the shotgun at me and stepping aside, out of the doorway. There was nothing I could do but sidle carefully past her into the kitchen, ever mindful of that gun she held.

'Stop. Wait there a minute,' she said when I had reached the back door. I waited while she retrieved a couple of rings of keys from a peg. Some of them were keys to the outboard, I supposed, though I couldn't guess what the others might be. She took time to slip on a jacket as well and pull the hood up over her hair.

'Okay, now, outside,' she said. 'We're going down to the dock, to the boat, but we're going to make a stop first at the toolshed.'

'The toolshed?' I asked. 'Where's the toolshed?'

'You'll see. Follow the path down toward the water. The toolshed is the little metal building just there, beside the path. About halfway down. I'll tell you when to stop.'

I obediently followed the path.

'Stop there,' she said.

I stopped just in front of small metal shed. 'It's padlocked,' I said.

'Here,' she said, tossing me a ring of keys.

Nervous, I dropped them and had to kneel down to pick them up off the wet ground. I thought I heard something behind us, and risked a glance beyond the woman with the shotgun, but there was only a bare bulb shining outside the back door. It provided a pale circle of light for a few feet beyond the door and nothing more. The rest of the yard was in deep shadows. I could see nothing. Probably, I thought, what I had heard had only been a raccoon or some other nighttime scavenger.

'Open it,' she said when I had gotten back to my feet with the keys, wiping my wet hands on my jeans. 'The brass key is the one to the padlock.'

It took me a moment of fumbling to get the padlock undone and the door open. When I had, she said, 'There should be a length of chain there, on the floor.'

'I see it.'

'Good. Get that.'

I did so. The chain was rusty and quite heavy. I managed to sling it over my shoulder, though I could not have carried it very far like that and I shuddered to think what that rust was doing to Sarah's poncho. Although if Anabelle was planning what I thought she was, I guessed that did not much matter.

'Now bring the chain with you,' she said, 'and lock the shed up again.'

With Anabelle keeping pace behind

205

me, I followed the path the rest of the way to their little dock at the lake end of their property. The boat with the outboard motor was moored there, tied to a piling. In the pale light I could see the waves on the surface of the water, making the small boat rock as if it wanted to be free from its restraints.

'What's the chain for?' I asked, hoping I had not already guessed the answer.

'You're going to wrap it around yourself a few times,' she said, 'before you go into the water.'

'I won't,' I said, but she seemed not even to hear my protest.

'That is, of course, because bodies float,' she said. 'But yours won't. The chain will keep you under long enough that there won't be anything left to identify you. The fish will go to work on you almost right away. Even if by some chance somebody should find you, and it's not likely to be anytime soon, they'll just think you're one of the people who died when that ferryboat sank years ago. After a body's spent some time in the water, it's hard to guess how long it's been there. And no one will have any reason to suspect the truth.'

'People will wonder why I just disappeared,' I said, but she seemed not to hear me.

We had come to the end of the dock. 'There,' she said, pointing with the shotgun. 'Climb into the boat. The front end.'

I threw the chain in first. The way the boat was rocking, I was half afraid it would toss me into the lake right here, and I did not want the chain to pull me under. Not yet, at least, though that certainly seemed what was in store for me, unless I could think of something clever to do. Just at the moment, I felt I was all out of ideas. I did manage, however, if a bit clumsily, to clamber into the boat. I got in midway along its length and scooted up to the front, leaving the chain where it was. It was unlikely, but there was always the chance that she might forget about it.

She got in after me, to the rear where the motor was, and a minute later the engine coughed to life. One-handed, keeping the shotgun more or less trained on me, she tossed off the ropes holding the boat to the dock, and a moment later we headed out onto the lake, into the darkness.

20

I sat frozen in fear. I thought I heard another boat somewhere not too far off, but in the dark, with the noise of the waves and the rain, it was impossible to be sure. I thought about shouting, screaming my head off; but even if there were someone else on the lake, and even if they heard me, who knew how long it would take them to find us. By that time, I might already be dead, shot and wrapped in my blanket of chains, and thrown overboard. I sat in terrified silence instead.

I don't even know how Anabelle knew where we were. It seemed to me as if we were going in circles, but I could not really say. Maybe she really was familiar enough with the lake that she did not need to see to know where she was going. I was not sure if that was a good thing.

We had ridden for some minutes in silence, so when she began to speak, out of the blue as it were, it made me jump. 'What I said back there,' she said as if she had been mulling this over for some time, and perhaps she had, 'about taking care of my mother. You know, that was just talk. Angry talk.'

'I knew that,' I said, thinking that after all I might get out of this alive.

'That wasn't why I . . . ' She hesitated. 'That wasn't why all this happened. She remembered something, is what it was. Something she saw. Or halfway remembered it, anyway. One minute it was clear in her mind, and the next it was gone. That's how her memory is these days. Or was. Things came to her and then they went. Seems there was no rhyme or reason to it.'

'It happens that way,' I said. I hesitated, afraid that I might rile her up again, and thinking too that if she talked things through, she might change her mind about what she had planned. Which was the safer course: to keep quiet, or to encourage her to talk? 'What did she see?' I asked, taking the bull by the horns.

She blinked and looked down the boat

at me as if she had never seen me before. 'That night,' she said, 'when I . . . you know, the girl and all that business. Later, afterward, when I got home, I came in the back way, through the back porch. I'd left the light on there when I went out for my walk. I always did, in case everyone else was asleep when I got back. So as not to disturb anyone. And as soon as I got into the light, I saw all the blood. On my clothes, on my hands, everywhere. It must have splattered when I . . . when she died. That's where our washer is, and the dryer, on the back porch, and there's a big old laundry sink out there too. Anyway, when I saw the blood, I stripped off my clothes, right down to my underwear, and I threw everything in the washer and got that running.

'But then I saw that it wasn't just my clothes. The baseball bat was bloody, too. So I was washing that in the big sink when my mother came out onto the back porch. 'Anabelle,' she said, surprised to see me back there in my skivvies. And then she saw the bat, and that sink full of bloody water, and the clothes in the washer, and she just said, 'Oh,' and went back inside. I don't think she grasped the significance then of what she'd seen. But I knew as soon as she heard about what had happened that she would put it all together. Her mind was still okay then.'

'And she must have known that it had been you who did it.'

'She did. Not then, but later certainly. And she meant to tell you about it, I knew she did. That was why I took her phone away from her, because she'd started calling you. By this time her memory had started to fail, she'd remember and then just as fast forget again. But I knew as sure as anything that one of these times you'd be there when she remembered, and once she told you, well, it'd all be over for me. That was why she had to die.' She paused for a moment, and added, 'That's why you have to die too.'

It was a long speech, and it filled me with terror. She had spoken so calmly. This was not a person in a panic, but a cold-blooded murderer.

In the next moment, a bolt of lightning

tore open the sky, and the rain began to come down hard, really hard, in torrents. Anabelle lifted one hand to shield her eyes, staring into the darkness, darker yet after that brilliant flash. She must have been looking for something to give her direction.

'Ahoy, there,' a voice came out of the darkness. 'Lake patrol. You, in the outboard. Identify yourself.' A beam of light slid back and forth across the water, making a valiant effort to pierce the darkness, but in the storm it looked no more than the flash of a match.

'It's me, Anabelle Gladstone,' she yelled back.

'You're not supposed to be out on the lake after dark without lights.'

'I've got them,' Anabelle shouted. 'I just didn't think they were needed. Nobody else is likely to be out here in this kind of weather.'

'They might be. And they might be running dark just like you are. Maybe we should lead you back in?'

'No, I'm all right. There, see.' She flicked on a running light. 'I'll head back in. No need for an escort.'

They seemed to be drifting away. The light got dimmer and the sound of their engine faded. Anabelle still held the shotgun in one hand, her left one. I knew she was right-handed. I found myself wondering how quickly she could raise that gun and aim it with only her left hand. Unfortunately, with a shotgun, I was pretty sure the aim did not have to be precise. The shots came out in a spray, meaning anywhere in the general neighborhood would do.

The rescue I had thought was at hand had gone. The only hope I had was to use my wits. I sat up suddenly in my end of the boat, my eyes wide. 'Listen,' I cried. 'Did you hear that?'

'What?' She gave me a blank look. 'The lake patrol? No, they've gone. That's their light over there, moving away. I think they've lost us.'

'No, not them. There it is again. Did you hear it?'

'Hear what?'

'It sounded like . . . it sounded like someone crying for help.'

'That's ridiculous. There's nobody out here but us and them, and they've gone, I tell you. And trust me, the lake patrol is not yelling for help.'

I skipped a beat, and said, my eyes ever wider, 'Then it must be the ghosts! The ghosts of the lake.'

'Baloney,' she said. 'There ain't no such thing.' But her eyes were wide, too, and she cocked her head, listening.

'I heard them, clear as anything,' I insisted. 'I tell you, it's them. There, I heard them again. 'Help us! Help us!' That's what they're crying.'

'I don't hear a thing.'

'Lean this way. You could hear them too if you were over here. You're too far away. Or it's the wind drowning them out for you.'

'You're foolin' me,' she said, but she did as I suggested and leaned toward me. For a moment, she had forgotten all about the gun.

It's now or never, I told myself, and suddenly bending one knee, I kicked at her hard. My shoe caught her shin, just below the left knee.

'Ow, damn you,' she cried, and started to raise the gun.

If she got that aimed in my direction, I was done for. In desperation, I kicked again, aiming this time for the shotgun, and this time my aim was true. My foot caught the gun and it flew out of her hands and went over the side of the boat. It hit the water with a loud splash.

But gun or no gun, I did not fancy a wrestling match anywhere, anytime, with Anabelle, and certainly not in the confines of a small boat. Which left me only one choice: to get out of the boat. I quickly rose up on my knees and dived over the side. A few seconds later, I hit the water in the wake of the shotgun.

It was like diving into a washing machine. The water churned and swirled, and it seemed in the first few seconds as if I had swallowed half the lake. I went under, and somehow managed to break the surface again, only to be slapped in the face by an angry wave. Again I went under.

It looked as if all I had done was jump from the frying pan into the fire. I had no clue where we were now in relation to the shore, and it could not have mattered greatly. Even if I had known where the shore was, I knew by now that I had no hope of swimming to it. The water was cold and toppling me end over end. I might have been a rag doll. *Lord*, I prayed, *you'll have to get me out of this somehow, because I sure can't do it for myself.*

And just at that moment, the strangest thing happened. It felt as if something, or someone, lifted me up. For a fleeting moment I was above the surface of the water. Not only could I breathe in air instead of water, but I could see lights in the near distance as well. Houses, windows, I thought. So we were not so far from the shore after all. *Well, girl*, I told myself, *you've got nothing to lose for trying.* I kicked off my shoes and began swimming toward those lights for all I was worth.

Within minutes, my arms felt like they had turned to lead. It was useless. I was a competent enough swimmer, but I could not swim that far in these stormy waters. I put my head back the way I had been taught years before in swim class, back at Miss Parker's, and let my feet drop, trying to float vertically long enough to catch my breath.

My right foot grazed bottom. A sandy bottom. I was over a sandbar. One of those Sarah had spoken of, built up from the sand scoured from the shore. If the sandbar was big enough, wide enough, maybe I could wade in, or at least part of the way in, till the sand ran out. It was worth a try, at least. When the alternative is dying, almost anything is worth a try. I put both feet down. Yes, both of them touched the sandy bottom. I started to walk, struggling against the pull of the water, paddling my hands but more to keep me upright than with any hope of gaining momentum.

'You bitch,' I heard a shout behind me. 'You come back here, you hear me, Beth Nolan? You come back here.'

It was Anabelle, cursing me. The outboard motor roared as she gunned it. I turned back and the boat's headlight hit me full in the face. She aimed the boat straight at me and came at a breakneck pace. If the boat hit me at that speed, it would slice me in two, and there was certainly no chance of my outrunning it.

But even if she knew what Sarah had tried to show me about the sandbars, I knew as well that in the dark she could not see the danger. 'Anabelle, no, it's too shallow here. I'm standing on a sandbar,' I tried to shout, and got a mouthful of water for my trouble.

The wind carried what little sound I made away. Anabelle was leaning forward in the boat, holding the chains aloft in one hand like she meant to beat me with them. In another flash of lightning, I could see the years of anger, of hatred, written across her face. Her eyes actually appeared to flash with the fire from above. The boat's headlight stayed in my face, growing bigger and bigger as she rushed toward me, pinning me where I was like a needle through a butterfly.

She hit the sandbar at full speed. For a few seconds, everything seemed to stand still. Then the boat rose up into the air like a balloon taking flight. I heard her scream and saw her clinging desperately to the sides of the boat before it flipped over. She was flung into the water, and an instant later, the upside-down boat came crashing down upon her.

I was sure the blow must have killed her. No one could have survived that violent crash and lived. But that did not save me. Unless some miracle occurred, I was soon going to be joining her in her watery grave. I tried once more to wade toward the shore, and after only a few steps, my feet slipped off the sand, and I was once again plunged into deep water. I had come to the end of the sandbar.

I sank once more beneath the surface, and this time I knew there was no hope for me. My consciousness was already fading.

Then suddenly I saw what looked at first like a curtain of white. It was hands, scores of them, skeletal hands, eerie white hands, reaching for me. The ghosts, surely, and this time I had no need to pretend. These were real, and it seemed they meant to claim me as one of their own.

Only, they were not dragging me down into the watery depths where they had lain for more than half a century. Instead, they were lifting me up, up and still further up. In another moment my head was above water, and I could breathe precious air. I gasped at it for all I was worth.

Then more hands, different hands this time, not the ghostly white ones of moments before, but flesh and blood hands, had hold of me. They were lifting me up.

'It's okay,' someone said, 'you're safe now. We've got you.'

I thought for a fleeting moment I knew that voice, but before I could figure out who it was, the blackness had taken me. I fainted.

$\star \quad \star \quad \star$

I was lying on my back. Someone was pressing hard at my chest, again and again, rhythmically. I took a big gulp of air and turned my head to the side, barely in time. I barfed. Seriously barfed. It seemed like gallons of water came out of me, out of my gaping mouth, out of my nose. For all I could say, even out of my ears.

'That's good,' a male voice said, 'Bring it up, all of it.'

When I finished retching, which might have been a minute or so, or hours for all I could say, I rolled onto my back again, gasping for breath, and opened my eyes. And there was Deputy Willis, leaning over me, his expression anxious. He saw my eyes flutter open and smiled, revealing those awful gaps in his teeth.

'You're awake. She's awake by damn it,' he said to someone else. 'You did a great job, Presley.'

Presley, apparently, was the woman who had been pressing on my chest. She was sitting back now on her heels with a relieved smile. I glanced at her and saw the uniform of the lake patrol.

'But how . . . what . . . ?' I was having difficulty forming words, but Willis seemed to understand my questions. Just maybe, I thought, he wasn't as goofy as he seemed.

'I saw her taking you out of the house,' he said. 'Anabelle. But she had that shotgun at your back. I was afraid if I tried to shoot her, she was going to shoot you. Just as a reflex action, you know what I mean? Anyhow, I couldn't shoot her in the back. So when I saw the two of you get into the boat and head out, I skedaddled down the road to fetch the lake patrol.'

'We've been on alert since the storm started,' Presley said. 'We always are when it storms.'

'We were out there looking for you,' Willis continued, 'back and forth across the lake, when we found the boat. But we lost you almost as fast. We'd just found you again when we saw you in the water and Anabelle comin' after you like hellfire and damnation. We tried to get there in time, but with the storm and all . . . ' His voice trailed off.

'Did she survive the crash?' I asked. 'Anabelle?'

'We haven't found her yet,' Willis said. 'But I don't hold out much hope. That boat came down on her like a ton of

223

bricks. To be honest, I halfway thought we'd lost you too, till you came up to the surface. Like a beach ball, you was, the way you was bobbing around in that water.'

I struggled to sit up. 'Hands,' I managed to say. 'I wasn't bobbing around. There were hands helping me, lifting me up.'

'That was us,' Willis said. 'Me and Presley here. I got to say, you were a slippery bundle to hold on to, all them wet clothes and everything. Next time you go for a swim, you might want to think of getting rid of some of that stuff.'

'I'll remember that,' I said, hoping that there would never be a next time.

'If it'd been me alone,' he said, 'I doubt I could've done it, but once Presley here got ahold of your jacket, there was no letting go. She won't give up.'

'I was determined,' Presley said.

'No, no, I have to tell you,' I said, and then checked myself. Maybe I had only imagined those white ghostly hands. I had been close to drowning. Maybe I had only hallucinated them. Anyway, who was likely to believe me?

'Thank you,' I finished lamely. 'That's what I wanted to tell you. Thank you both.'

Whatever I had experienced in the water, it was probably better if I kept it to myself. After all, they already called Lake Caspar 'Ghost Lake.'

I did not need to add to the stories.